The Oriphate

THE ORIPHATE

by

DW Cantrell

DORRANCE PUBLISHING CO., INC.
PITTSBURGH, PENNSYLVANIA 15222

ISBN # 0-8059-6900-4
Printed in the United States of America

First Printing

For information or to order additional books, please write:
Dorrance Publishing Co., Inc.
701 Smithfield Street
Third Floor
Pittsburgh, Pennsylvania 15222
U.S.A.
1-800-788-7654

Or visit our web site and on-line catalog at
www.dorrancepublishing.com

My Beginnings

Before this all started, I was just regular old Robert Stevens. I never would have thought that I was special. I don't mean special as in getting a brand-new car on your sixteenth birthday. Nor do I mean I was special as in strawberry ice cream on Sunday afternoon after church. I mean special in a way that cannot be described in one or two sentences or even in a week's time. I must tell you the whole story in order for you to fully understand it all, because if someone would have told me flat out, I would not have believed it myself.

I was born on June 19, 1939, in Springhare, Iowa. I was born to a very young mother who ran a small store. I never met my father because he was killed in World War II. Well, I guess I did meet him, but I was much too young to remember him. I had several photographs of him that I kept in my room, one in which he was in uniform. He was a lieutenant stationed in North Africa for some time as I understand, but was later relocated. He was killed in a German air raid that took place in London only weeks before the war ended.

I was barely six years old when my father was brought back stateside and buried. I don't remember a whole lot about it, but I do remember my mother's telling me that he died fighting for freedom. She would often tell me how brave he was, and that he would have been perfectly happy dying in battle. Apparently, that was the greatest admiration any man or woman for that matter could have had, I suppose—to die in a courageous manner. It seems that just a plain old death wasn't quite as adventurous or honorable as dying for some great cause.

Everyone in town seemed to worship my father. Well, they didn't really worship him, but they thought a lot of him. They also thought a lot of my grandfather. He was a strict man who served in the military as well. He fought in World War I, but he was not allowed to serve during World War

II, because he owned a lumberyard. Much of his lumber was sold to the Allied forces and used overseas, and he was quite happy to be doing this.

His name was Robert, just like me, and he was a very firm man. He was especially strict with my mother, or so she says. She had been running a store that the family owned since she was fifteen years old, and she had very little time to socialize. My father would often come and visit her at the store before they were wed. My mother loved running the store though, because much like her father, she enjoyed seeing the fruits of her own labor. It gave her an incredible feeling of self-worth. I understand she took it quite hard when she heard that my father had died, but nevertheless, she was very strong, and she was back running the store rather quickly.

I had lots of fun in that store as a young boy. Seeing all the townspeople was very interesting. I knew practically everyone in town by the time I was eight years old. I would often help around the store and listen to all the stories the townsfolk would tell about my father. It seems that he was quite the Tom Sawyer in his day. The only person who ever dared speak ill of my father was his father-in-law, Grandpa. He didn't really understand the adventurous attitude my father had, and anytime someone would tell a wild store about him, my grandfather would just look off and mumble things to himself.

My grandfather took his role in the military a bit more seriously than my father did, or so he says. Grandpa didn't really see war as a way to be an adventurer. He saw it as more of a job like any other with greater circumstances. He always claimed that my father joined the military just to see the world and kill Germans, but Grandpa claimed that his service in World War I was a call to duty. I never really understood his argument, because it seemed that both their hearts were in the right place. It didn't really matter why either of them fought. What was more important is that they did fight.

My grandfather also owned a feed store there that had been in his family for three generations. I guess you could say the feed store was his baby. His saw mill was just a part-time venture, and he sold it not long after the war ended. During his service in the military, my grandmother and various hired help had to run the feed store and did quite well, or she says so, but grandfather thought otherwise.

When I turned fourteen, or a few months after I turned fourteen rather, my mother contracted whooping cough. At first it seemed like a plain old cold, and it was quite easy to catch a cold working around everyone in town. Well, the cold took a turn for the worse, I guess you would say, and whooping cough set in by winter. She eventually had to be hospitalized, and she got worse and worse. The doctors told us, if she could have made it until spring, she would have had a better chance, but she died in late February. It was quite sad, but I knew she wouldn't want me to mope around and cry every day, so I didn't. I just accepted it.

I had to move in with my grandparents, and that was quite a different situation. However, my grandfather was not as strict on me as he was on my mother. I later learned that parents were much stricter on daughters than they were on sons in those days. Nevertheless, I got along quite well with both my grandparents.

Grandpa sold the general store to an aspiring young businessman named Mitch Medallion, and I was not too happy about that. There was nothing I could do about I, though, so I let that go as well. I missed the store the most of all. I hated the fact that I couldn't see everyone at the store and hear all the stories they would tell, but soon enough I was working at the feed mill.

My grandfather wanted me to take over the family business, and I was quite happy to do so. He felt that it was my birthright, and I agree wholeheartedly. It was tough, however, because I had to work really hard to learn everything I needed to know to run the place on my own. By the time I was sixteen, I could virtually run the whole place by myself, but I only worked after school and on Saturdays. The weekdays were not nearly as bad. I learned most of what I needed to know on Saturdays, but my grandfather was not quite ready to let me run the mill by myself. He would find any little thing to correct me on, but they were few and far between.

It was not until I had graduated high school in the spring of '55 that my grandfather let me run the mill by myself. He would still pop in every few days and inspect everything to see if it was to his liking. He seemed to be pleased most of the time and the patrons seemed to enjoy my service, and all the hands seemed to like me as well. I was quite happy myself. I really enjoyed working with the public and running my own business. It seemed to be what I was meant to do, and I thanked my mother, because she was quite the businesswoman herself. I knew she would have been proud of me.

That summer was one of the best times of my life. Not only had I done exceptionally well at the feed store, but I had met a wonderful girl named Sumer, which was fitting because we met in the summer. She was still in high school, and she was the niece of a farmer who had known my family for years. He seemed to think it was a respectable young businessman, and he did not mind our making social calls on one another. We had so much fun that summer that we hardly noticed it slowly fading away. As it came to an end, Sumer had to go back to her home in Illinois, and we promised to keep in touch. I wrote her two days after she left, but I never received her reply.

The Stranger

The morning my adventure started was just like any other at the feed store. I arrived there around four o'clock that morning to make sure that everything was ready for the long day ahead of me and my employees. It seemed as if it was going to be a beautiful day. Even though the sun wasn't up yet, I could tell from the chirping robins that the weather was going to be sunny and delightful. I had quite a spring in my step for some reason, and I whistled as I walked past the counter. I loved the month of September more than any month because the weather was always so pleasant. I loved fall so very much.

I walked around the storage room of the feed mill, checking to make sure everything was in place and ready to go. I already knew that John Maddox, a local pig farmer, was coming to buy a week's supply of corn because he had run out the day before, and I was expecting a shipment of dry peas that afternoon, and there had to be plenty of room for them as well.

As you can suspect, exciting things rarely ever happened in Springhare, nor did anyone expect them to, but that morning the most exciting thing that could happen to anyone happened to me. The adventure started around five o'clock that morning, and it was quite a shock. I was simply walking around out back of the storage mill, smoking a cigarette, when I heard a noise. I figured it was Richard or someone else who worked at the feed mill looking for me, but I was very wrong. I walked back inside the building and headed slowly back toward the front.

"Hello," I called out, "Rich, is that you?" No one answered. "Hello, Larry, Rich, is that you? Where are you?" As those words left my mouth, I heard the noise again. It was like footsteps. Someone was in the storage room with me. "If this is a joke, ha-ha. This isn't funny, guys. Now come on out." By that time, I had picked up a small metal pipe that had been lying around, because I was a little frightened. After a few seconds of silence, a voice spoke from behind.

"Good morrow, sir."

I turned around swiftly to find a man about my size wearing a hooded cloak of some kind, carrying a large stick.

"Who are you?"

"My name is Seravin."

"You've about scared the hell out of me, and furthermore, you are not supposed to be back here."

"Sir, are you Robert Charles Stevens?"

"Yes, what do you want with me?"

"Good, I am so glad that I found you. You must come with me immediately," he said as he passed me rather quickly.

"Go with you where? I can't go with you."

"You have no choice; you must."

"Ah—no, I do have a choice, and I am most certainly not going anywhere. I have a business to run here and I..."

"You are needed in a far away place now at this very moment. You are larger and more important than this reality. You must come now."

"Are you some kind of lunatic? Reality? What are you saying?"

"I can't tell you now, because you wouldn't believe me, but you are coming one way or the other, even if I have to use force."

"Well, come on buddy. I have a little force of my own here. This pipe and I will knock you upside the head if I have to."

Upon saying this, the strange fellow uttered words from his mouth that sounded inhuman, and a bolt of light sprang from his mouth. I don't really remember what happened after that, except for lying facedown on the floor. I immediately jumped to my feet, and the man was gone.

The next ordeal started as soon as I got up, and I really don't know how to describe it at all, but I'll try. It seems that a large glowing ball of light that started as a speck appeared before me. I watched it grow bigger and bigger, and the bigger it got, the stronger it became. Soon there was a windstorm blowing in the storage room. I could hardly stand for all the powerful wind that was blowing around me. Then things started flying into the light. I watched the metal pipe I had been holding fly right into the light and disappear, along with bags of corn, pallets, and various other objects. Soon enough I was airborne and flying toward the light, and I flew right into the light.

I then found myself along with all the objects that had been with me, flying through what appeared to be a tunnel composed of light, but it wasn't like a normal tunnel. I was flying through this tunnel as opposed to gliding along the side of it. It was quite a strange feeling. The next feeling was very familiar, however. I came to an abrupt stop, colliding into the ground, that is. I violently rolled along and eventually stopped looking up at what appeared to be a beautiful blue sky. I slowly got up, to say the least, and the morning seemed to be off to a wonderful start. I had just been flung through something that I never could have dreamed existed and was in a place I had never seen before in my life. In one direction there were huge snow-capped mountains, and in the other direction was a huge forest. One thing was for sure, I wasn't in Springhare.

The smell of salt filled the air, and I was almost sure that I could hear water. As I walked toward the brush and small trees in front of me, I looked around at the various array of tools and feed bags that had been smashed into the ground just as I was. I couldn't believe that I survived, because everything else was completely destroyed. Right in front of the trees was the pipe I had pulled on the figure in the storage room, stuck up in the ground (some protection that was).

Past the thick brush and vines that grew through the small path, I found myself looking at something I had never seen before. A giant ocean lay before me in all its greatness. Large waves as big as a three-story building crashed on the rocks that lay far out past where the shore ended. Now it was very clear that I was nowhere near Iowa.

Down the shore about twenty feet I saw the man who had brought me here, sitting next to a fire. He looked much more inviting with his hood down. He was a dark-complected individual with a small beard. It reminded me of those beards that New York businessmen grew. It started as a mustache and came down around his mouth into a small goatee. His hair was quite short in comparison to mine, and his face looked rugged and scarred.

Of course, I wasn't exactly pleased with him, to say the least, but considering the beautiful countryside, I could hardly be angry. I was also pretty sure that he could easily hit me with another one of those bolts, and I didn't really want that either.

"Well, hello again, dear boy," he stated aloud as he stood up. "I'm glad to see you made it. I am quite sorry about the trip. I hope it didn't frighten you too much."

"I can't lie. It was intense. I am at a loss for words—overwhelmed I guess you would say."

"Of course you are. Come sit down and I'll begin to try and tell you what you need to know for now, but it is going to be hard for you to understand."

I sat down next to the fire with the gentleman, and he offered me a warm drink. I figured it would be rude to refuse, so I took it. It was very much like coffee, but a great deal stronger.

"That is limela weed. It is a potent stimulant that you and I will need for the journey we are about to embark on. That's the only flaw in hyperdimensional travel. You never know where you will end up."

"Hyperdimensional?"

"Yes, you see, your dimension, or the Third Dimension I should say, is quite easy to navigate through. But this one is a great deal more complicated."

"So, exactly what dimension is this?"

"Let's don't worry about that right now. Let's think of it as another reality. You see, reality or anything that exists outside of perception is infinite—or I should say what we actually know is very small in comparison to what really exists."

"So, this is another planet?"

"You can think of it in that way, but not really. You see, this place—all of this around you—does not exist in your reality. The men of your world, Earth I suppose, could travel the lengths of the universe and never find it."

"Well, how did you find it or find me?"

"That is the key to the whole mess we are in right now and why I have brought you here."

"And that is?"

"You see, the inhabitants of this world, Aristrasia, as it is called, discovered a powerful energy flux thousands of centuries ago, and they used it as a fuel source. They never questioned where it came from or what made it; they just used the energy. Well, eventually the energy ran out, and the inhabitants left his world and spread out into the various planets near this one. Do you see that small green sphere in the western sky there?"

"Yes."

"That is Almotar. It is near a giant star called Genealation, which allows us to see it from here. Many inhabit that planet and have for thousands of years, but this was the beginning of all the civilizations that flourished here in this galaxy. About five hundred years ago, a group of scientists came to this planet once more and discovered another energy flux—one that greatly outpowered any that have ever been recorded. This positive energy force had completely changed what used to be a desolate wasteland into the flourishing ecosystem that you see before you."

"That sounds all well and good, but what's the catch and what does it have to do with me?"

"Hold on, I'll get to you in a minute. Well, the energy flux brought life back to the land of Aristrasia, so naturally people started resettling here, and as you said, it was fine until a group of madmen came here and started performing unsanctioned witchcraft."

"Witchcraft?"

"Yes, this ancient group of religious leaders came here in search of a place to perform and practice their beliefs. They promised to leave well enough along and practice their religion in secret, and the ruling body agreed. But it seems that the fools did something so disturbing, which none of us knows what, that opened another flux that killed everything within miles of the accident."

"So, the energy flux is causing the problem, correct?"

"Well, not exactly, but that is all I know about that, as of now."

"But you said you—"

"Would tell you how you fit into all of this."

"Yes."

"Well, I can tell you that, but I will have to tell you on the trail. We must make half the journey before nightfall. Here, you must eat these. They are a derivative of what you call carbohydrates—specifically glucose. I'm sure the travel here drained all your glycogen reserves, and you will need energy for the trip."

The things he handed me didn't look at all appetizing. They looked like small insects of some kind with only four legs as opposed to six with rather long wings.

"Excuse me," I said as he packed his things. "Are these bugs or something?"

"Oh, no. They used to be," he said comically as he snapped his fingers. As quick as he did this, the luminous fire that had been burning with such brightness went out in a spark and two flashes. He looked at me, and I know as well as he did that I must have looked as if I had seen a ghost.

"How did you do that?"

"The same way I turned those beetles into glucose. With magic."

AN OLD FRIEND

I was even more curious now about so many things, and I had thousands of questions running about in my mind. I had had the single most exciting day of my life, and yet it appeared that it was going to get more and more interesting as time went on. I had completely forgotten about the feed store and all my responsibilities and how angry my grandfather was going to be when he saw the storage room and that I was not there. I could just imagine the look on his face when he saw the room destroyed and over a thousand dollars of feed gone. I thought to myself, "He might just keel over when he sees it."

"Don't worry about your grandfather. I'm sure he is very worried about you rather than being worried about his business."

"How did you? Wait, can you hear my thoughts?"

"Not all of them, just the ones that are important."

"Are you some kind of psychic or what?"

"No, I am just a simple magician. You have the ability to do magic yourself, but I have had to train for years and study quite hard to learn my trade. I guess now is a good time to explain why you are hear and about your special gift."

"Come again. I though you said something about me doing magic."

"You are a very special being indeed, Robert Stevens. You possess a great power, and you are by far the most powerful being in this dimension, and I dare to say in yours as well. You are an Oriphate."

"An Oriphate?"

"Yes," he said has he turned toward me. "You have a genetic trait that allows you to attain powers that no one could possibly comprehend. Many studies have been done, and it is the opinion of most that you are the only one that has this trait."

"What do you mean trait?"

"On your thirteenth chromosome there is a base pair sequence that allows you to have limited powers in your reality, but the full extent of your powers can be brought to light here. This sequence is special, and you are the only creature in all existence that has it."

"Base pairs? Oh, you mean in my DNA."

"Yes, deoxyribonucleic acid."

"Well, I'll be damned. How do you know all of this?"

"You have Alder Dimms to thank for discovering this. He is a brilliant man who has studied you and your world quite extensively, especially human biochemical processes."

"Why?"

"I can't tell you that, because I do not know."

"They didn't tell you."

"No. I don't even know that much about hyperdimensional travel they discovered."

"I was thinking you did that with magic."

"Oh, no. That sort of thing could never be done with magic. I seriously doubt that you could do that as an Oriphate."

"I don't have any powers. I didn't even have 'limited' powers in my world."

"Yes, you did. You just didn't know you did."

"Name one."

"Well, didn't you ever find it funny that you would know things before they happened? Dream things one night, and then watch them happen the next day."

"I always thought that was coincidental."

"No, you knew there were going to happen before they did—the most important one being the death of your mother."

"I did dream about it several times before she got sick. Sometimes I feel as if I should have…"

"No, never feel that way. There is nothing you could have done, because you cannot change the future nor can you change the past. If you ever do, things will turn out worse than they would if you didn't. Trust me."

"What difference does it make? If I had the chance to go back and save my mother, I would."

"No, you don't understand. By going back and saving your mother, you could be destroying something else, or disrupting any other natural event that would have taken place. Even by being in the past, you could alter the future by simply stepping on a flower or talking to someone. It is best just to leave the past alone."

"Well, how am I supposed to use these powers? I don't really feel any different."

"That is not important now. What is important is that we get to the Piper before nightfall. He will provide us with shelter and hopefully a hot meal."

I was quite shocked to discover that I was an Oriphate and magic was real. I had been told all my life that magic wasn't real, and now I have seen that magic could be done and that it was very real.

As we walked on, I had an uneasy feeling come over me. It felt as if someone had dropped me into ice-cold water. I had the strangest feeling that we were in danger. This warning signal continued to flash in my head, and it got stronger and stronger.

"Avin, I don't feel right. Something's wrong."

"Well, I can see that I brought the right person. Yes, there is a Cravenor about somewhere."

"What the hell is a cravenor?"

"It's a cursed cave dwelling creature that preys on the weak and eats children."

"You're kidding, right?"

"No, I'm quite serious, but don't be alarmed. It won't attack us as long as you are here."

"Why not?"

"Because like all other damned creatures that are found in places that are not cursed, they fear such strong powers. He feels exactly the same way you do right now, and he knows there is no chance of defeating you."

"What if it were only you, making the journey alone?"

"I would have to fight it off, of course. I had to slay one during the third trial, so I'm sure I would manage."

Knowing it wouldn't attack us made me feel a little bit better, but I still didn't understand how I was any different from anyone else or from Avin for that matter. He seemed to be exactly homologous to most humans I had ever seen. How was he any different? I had to figure this out, but conversation time was over for now.

Suddenly I started feeling strange again, but it was a different kind of feeling. A small man wearing a green suit was dancing about in my head playing a small flute. The music was quite soothing, and it made me feel very relaxed. It was the most relaxed I had felt in some time. It was a very queer feeling. Avin soon interrupted my thoughts.

"We are here," Avin called out from ahead. It seems that I had fallen behind but not too far behind.

"Look, there is the Piper's home."

And there sat a little man I had seen in my thoughts. I tell you, I wasn't feeling like myself at all, and it was getting worse the farther we went.

"Seravin, you old magic maker. What brings you this deep into the forest and by it all, in the opposite direction?"

"I have just returned from the Third Dimension with a friend. This is Robert Stevens."

"Oh my, is it really him? Oh my, it is."

With that, the Piper bowed down before me and gracefully reached out and took my hand.

"It is a pleasure to meet the great Oriphate. I wish you the best of luck on your quest, friend."

"Thank you. Do stand up."

"Yes, forgive me. You two must come inside and stay the night. The woods are just crawling with night ghouls and evil things. Come in."

The Piper had a quaint home, and it glowed with friendliness. You just felt at home there, or I did anyway. The hollowed-out tree that he lived in was a great deal larger than any of the trees I had ever seen.

"You two have traveled all the way from the shore of Norana."

"Yes, it was quite a journey."

"Avin, you must tell me of the Third Dimension. What wonders did you see there?"

"Well, no offense Robert, but it wasn't all that amazing."

"None taken," I said lightheartedly. "You're right. It is boring compared to this world."

"Oh, nonsense. A place that harnesses such energy must be brilliant."

"Excuse me," I said curiously.

"The energy flux from the Third Dimension that has us in peril. These two fluxes originate in your reality."

"Yes, Piper," Avin said with an interesting tone. "I was told that you had a great deal to tell us about these matters. I am curious to hear what you know."

"First, let us eat, and then I will tell you everything I have heard."

After dinner we all sat comfortably around a warm fire that Avin had started in the stove. I was well and ready to hear what the Piper had to say. It was all I could do not to ask him during the meal, but I knew that would have been rude. I did find out that the Piper was a magician much like Avin, and his flute was enchanted. This is what allowed him to remain safe this deep in the woods. It seems that the flute could ward off danger and restore life to those of pure heart, a task that was tested on Avin as a young boy.

"Well, friends, I have been told many things, as I am often by travelers and fools that pass through here, but none as interesting as what a traveler told me a few weeks ago. He claimed to be close to the inner circle of the researchers killed a few years ago."

"The ones killed at the negative flux."

"Yes, he claimed to have known several of them. He also told me of the research the scientist in Albera had used to send you to the Third Dimension. He claimed to know Alder."

"That's strange. Alder has not spoken of any such man, but he knows much more than he tells any of us. I wouldn't doubt that this man tells the truth."

"He told me many things about the problem that we face. He was quite convincing."

"Well, what of the negative flux and the scientist?"

"Both fluxes are coming from the Third Dimension. It seems, or so the traveler says, that neither of the fluxes is positive or negative. The fact that there are two of them has caused the problem. The two fluxes together have caused a shift in the time space continuum, and this is what has caused the distress in Elberion."

"Forgive me, Piper, but am I to understand that the energy is coming from Earth?" I asked with great interest.

"Earth?"

"Robert's reality."

"Yes, the Third Dimension, right."

"And what do you mean distress?"

"Well, the energy flux, the negative one that is, has destroyed Elberion. This is the state closest to the flux, and it will soon destroy the entire realm."

"Well, what do we do?" I asked.

"That is where you come in, young Oriphate. You will attempt to complete the sixth, and seventh trials."

"What does that mean?"

"Well," the Piper replied, "it simply means that you must travel into the positive flex, and this will give you the power to destroy the negative flux, or so the traveler said."

"Will that not kill me?"

"It seems that your 'genetic makeup' as the traveler called it can allow you to do this."

"What makes my genetics different from yours or Avin's?"

"You are composed of carbon-based molecules much like the energy that flows here from the Third Dimension. It seems that carbon is the backbone of your entire reality, but you see we are composed of a material that in no way compares to the materials you are made of. It is your DNA that allows you to be an Oriphate, where we could never do so. Alder Dimms has studied the energy that flows from your dimensions, and he has used it to create magic as well as the hyperdimensional travel that brought you here, but the energy had to converted to another form. You can walk right up to either flux, where we would simply be destroyed."

"Is that why the scientists were killed?" Avin asked.

"Well, that's a good question. The traveler seemed to think they were far enough from the flux to be safe."

"So he thinks they were killed," I said with curiosity.

"He didn't say, but the tone in his voice did suggest foul play."

Avin scratched his beard for a moment and spoke.

"Alder has spoken of these things, but not in great detail. It is possible that this man knows more than he is saying. Do you think he was a spy?"

"No, I am sure he is pure at heart, but nonetheless, he still seemed to be hiding something."

"What you are telling us scares me, Piper, because this man has told you things that we are unsure of, and there is also the chance that the man is right. Those researchers could have been murdered."

"Well, should we be worried?"

"Don't worry. You have a brilliant guide who knows these woods better than anyone. He will get you to Alder, safe and sound."

"But I am afraid that I will not be able to destroy what is causing this world to die."

"Robert, do you feel the least bit different since you arrived here?"

"Yes, I do feel strange. I can hear, see, and smell much better. I don't really understand it."

"It is because we grow closer to the energy flux. The closer we get to the flux, the stronger you get. You will soon harness the full potential of your powers. Piper, you have been a great help to us, and it grows late. If we are to leave at the break of dawn, we must get some sleep."

"Yes, that would be a good idea."

The next morning we left not long before the sun rose. It looked as if it was going to be a tad cloudy, but you could hardly see the light for the thick limbs overhead. As we walked along, I pulled out a cigarette and lit it. I puffed it as I walked alongside Avin, I noticed him eyeing the cigarette, just as he had yesterday. He seemed to be amazed by it.

"Robert, what are these smoking sticks you have? They seem strange to me."

"This? Why it is a cigarette. It is made of tobacco, which is a plant that grows in my dimension."

"It just seems strange to me that you would willingly inhale smoke. Isn't that dangerous?"

"They are starting to say that it can kill you, but not everyone dies from it."

"That seems like a frightening chance to take."

"I understand. My grandmother feels the same way about it, but my grandfather smokes two packs a day. You are not so different from people in my dimension, you know."

"I guess everyone takes chances sometimes, but we never really think about it until it affects us directly. You could say that walking through these woods is a dangerous chance to take."

We walked on through the woods. We went over fallen trees, through thick limbs and vines, around huge rocks, and up hills covered in what appeared to be ferns and other various bushes that I could not identify. As we went along, I started to notice every living thing around me, from every bug to every songbird. I could hear the beautiful songs before they even started. It was almost as if I could hear the trees growing around me. The rays of light that shot through the trees appeared different as well. I was able to see the waves of light energy bouncing to and fro as they made their way down from millions of miles away in space. I was totally and completely emerged in the ecosystem, and it ran through my veins to my heart, around my body and back again.

But this feeling of content sharply turned to dismay, and the wonderful feelings in which I had been so deeply imbedded drained down to nothingness. My mood turned black as night, and the void drained me. When I felt this come over me, it almost brought me to my knees. Looking around at the surroundings, I noticed that everything around me was bleak and lifeless.

"Avin, this place disturbs me deeply. What happened here?"

"I was hoping we would miss it completely, but we're going right through the edge of it. This is a cursed place. Something very bad happened here years ago, but no one is sure what. Rumor has it that the witches did some of their most evil black magic here before they were killed. We must be extremely careful here. Keep all your senses alert. There are things here that will attack anything that moves," and before Avin could finish, a creature came from somewhere, where I'm not sure, and knocked Avin clear out of sight. It appeared to be walking on all fours, but I couldn't tell because I was scared. It crawled along smelling the ground where Avin stood. The face on the creature was a sight that could have killed. It seemed to be double-jointed, and it was equipped with four long arms and three-inch claws. After kneeling and sniffing a bit, it made its way towards me. Once it was within a foot of me, it rose up and drew one of its long arms intending to deliver a fatal strike.

Then, just as fast as a light switch or the blink of an eye, the creature went flying through the air ten times faster than Avin had flown. After smacking into a tree and falling twenty feet to the ground, the creature ran off, yelping all the way. The yelps slowly faded away, and to my surprise, Avin was just coming to his knees.

"Avin, I thought you did that."

"No," he said coughing a bit, "I think you did that, and it is quite amazing indeed."

"I can't believe I did that. I wasn't even, I mean, well. You..."

From the looks of it, and believe me, I didn't get a very good look at the creature, but I think it was an Orgatandor. It's a beast conceived from pure fear and hatred, which in turn feeds on fear and malice. It empowers the beast."

"So how on earth did I do that? I assure you that I was scared to death just then. I saw the monster knock you clean off your feet."

"Yes, and I'm quite lucky he didn't kill me. But I don't think it was here for either of us."

"Well, who then?"

"I don't know. Come, we must go quickly before it returns."

"I am starting to feel life again. We must be near the end."

"Yes, we are very close."

So we hurried along and soon came back into the living forest, and it was much more peaceful. I was happy to hear living creatures again, but I wondered how I had defeated the creature. I had to know.

"Avin, how did I defeat the Orgatandor?"

"It is quite simple. You just wanted the creature as far away from you as possible, and that is exactly what happened."

"You mean I did that with my thoughts?"

"Not just your thoughts, but your subconscious thoughts."

"What do you mean?"

"Your subconscious or the thought displayed during sleep."

"Oh, you mean like dreams."

"Yes."

"But I was awake."

"Do you remember what I told you about reality?"

"Yes. Reality is anything that exists when you can't see it."

"Yes. Those thoughts still exist, even when you're awake. Subconscious thoughts are a great deal of what Oriphates use, as opposed to magicians, who use conscious thoughts. That is why our powers are so limited."

"Wait a minute. That's how you can hear my thoughts?"

"Yes, I can hear your conscious thoughts."

"Then how do you know what I was thinking about when the creature was about to attack me?"

"I don't. You had no conscious thoughts. Remember, I can hear conscious thoughts, and that was an important time for me to hear your thoughts. There were none."

"That makes sense, because I wasn't really thinking about a whole lot at the time. I was scared out of my wits."

"Yes, and your subconscious mind kicked in and saved you."

With that I pulled Avin back. "Do you feel that?"

"No, I don't feel anything."

"Up ahead."

As we walking along, the strange feeling grew stronger, steadily overtaking me. It was an eerie sensation. I had not yet had an awareness such as this, and it felt quite different from anything I had come to know in since I had arrived in the world of Aristrasia. I couldn't reasonably say what it was, but I knew it wasn't good. I could sense something or someone near us, but it was...

"Look there," Avin said as he walked ahead. "It is a man."

"He's dead." Apparently, the man had been killed sometime ago. His throat was slit wide open, and he was starting to decompose.

"I wonder who this is."

"This is the gentleman that the Piper spoke of."

"How do you know that, Robert?"

"I don't really understand how I know, but it is him."

Avin felt around in the main's pockets in hopes of finding something that would allude to his identity or a clue that could possibly lead to a motive.

"Whoever killed this man cleaned his pockets out and took whatever he was carrying his things in. He has absolutely nothing on him."

"I think he knew too much, but I wonder where the fellow that killed him is?"

"Well, let's not stick around to find out. We're not far from Granate. The sooner we get there the better."

So we headed on up the path. I didn't feel right about just leaving the man in the woods without a proper burial, but I suppose we were a little more pressed for time now, considering there was a killer in the woods somewhere. It didn't really scare me, though, because defeating the creature back in the cursed zone made me much more confident about my powers. I could sense the flux drawing closer, and it was a wonderful experience. I could hardly understand it myself.

I guess we were about two hundred yards from Granate when something really disturbing happened. At first, I became very weak but awake at the same time. Then I blacked out, but it was like I was still awake in another place. It felt just like I had apparated into another reality somewhere without even trying to. This place was very different from the woods. It was quite dark and damp, and a sentiment of despair filled the air around me, as several ghoulish figures passed me rather quickly. I noticed that they were not actually walking, but hovering over the ground. I soon realized that these creatures could neither see nor hear me.

They made their way to a large altar in the middle of a large, circular room. The hallway, from which I entered was only one of about ten entrances that ran all along the edge of the room. A great number of these creatures started entering the other doors and gathering around the altar, but I couldn't see what they were doing. At that exact moment I became airborne soaring through the air and eventually ending up facing down from the ceiling of the room. I slowly crept along the ceiling until I was directly over the altar, but I still couldn't tell what was going on. I started to wonder if I really wanted to know, but I was here for a reason. I was curious as to why I had been brought here, and I was sure that it would help us on our mission.

So I flew quite slowly toward the altar in order to get a better look. I must say that what I saw was very disturbing indeed. There was a girl lying naked on the altar, and she didn't seem to be breathing. There were tiny symbols carved and burned into her skin. These symbols covered her entire body. I covered my mouth in disgust as I approach the altar. Everything was becoming clearer, and I soon noticed that the girl's eyes had been removed. I thought to myself, *What manner of vile sadistic scum could do such a thing?* This sight was worse than any nightmare. It was a nightmare, but I couldn't wake up.

The creatures, which had been gathering around for what seemed like hours, had been silent until a low roar started to be uttered in a slight monotone sort of voice. I couldn't tell where it was coming from, but it was very close. The louder it got, the harder it was for me to concentrate on the events that were unfolding around me. As the low noise continued, the creatures all started to kneel from front to back, and the noise became more and more high-pitched. What had been a low roar quickly became a high screech. It got so high that I could hardly breathe. It was the kind of sound that would drive normal men insane. The noise came to a sudden climactic end, and the young girl sat up quicker than a bolt of lightening and let out a scream that could have woken the dead. A reflex of pure fright shot through my spine, and in desperation, I flew into the ceiling as fast as the girl had sprung from her deathbed. Almost jumping out of my skin in a cold sweat, I found myself sitting in a candle-lit room with Avin by my side.

"Are you all right, Robert?"

"I think so. Where are we?"

"We're in the castle of Lostine. You went into a trance about three hundred yards from the castle. I carried you here."

"I saw something. It was like a dream, but it was so real."

"What did you see? You must tell me before we meet with the council tomorrow."

A Most Unpleasant Surprise

The "palace" wasn't what I thought it would be. It resembled a medieval castle or a gothic cathedral a vampire would live in. The castle was cold and damp, and the ceilings were constantly leaking a murky, brownish liquid. I didn't have the sensation of warmth I had in the forest. It felt like a place of hate and malice. Evil seemed to leak from the ceiling as well. I could tell that bad things had happened there in the past.

We had been there for about three hours, and the only person I saw or spoke to was Avin. He explained that I had blacked out and had an out-of-body subconscious vision. He fully assured me that what I had seen was real, and it probably happened only hours before I viewed it in my mind. I thoroughly explained what I had seen in my dream state, and he said it would be best to meditate on it. Every once in awhile I would jerk violently once or twice, but Avin assured me that it would pass with time. He explained that my muscles had to relax, because they become very rigid during a vision. He warned me that some action potentials would result in a large amount of calcium flooding into my muscle cells as they readjusted to the normal amount. He seemed to know more about my body than I did.

This also gave me a little time to ponder what was happening in the Third Dimension. I had been gone several days now, and Grandma and Grandpa were probably worried sick. I also started to come to the realization that I didn't really owe these beings anything, or did I? I started to think about how the two fluxes were affecting Earth and the Third Dimension for that matter. If these two fluxes had put this dimension out of balance, it is possible they were putting the Third Dimension out of balance as well. After all, these two fluxes were coming from the Third Dimension, but where? It could be on Earth, or it is very possible it could be on Mars, or any other planet in the solar system. The sun could even have something to do with it. There were a lot of questions yet to be answered.

I was most disturbed by the vision I had earlier that day. It was the single most frightening thing I had ever seen or felt in my entire life. It scared me more than when I was told that my mother was going to die. I felt a little bad about it, but I was almost certain that my mother would have understood why it frightened me so. The young girl stood out in my mind and my every thought. I knew I would never forget such a sight, and I would see that girl's face every waking moment for the rest of my life. It also made me think about the horrors that were to come and the terrors that I would see in the coming days.

It was hard to imagine what these freaks were capable of doing. If someone could do that to a young girl, they clearly had no conscience whatsoever. I was more afraid then I had ever been, but at the same time I had never been so egotistical. I was having feelings of such great power running through me. It felt as if I could take on any challenge I was faced with, and even though I didn't know the girl in my vision, I wanted to avenge her death in some way. Someone had to be punished for this crime, and they would be.

I laid there awake in the small bed and tried to go to sleep. Avin had come by and brought my dinner. It was something that resembled soup with large chunks of something in it. He said they were a combination of triglycerides, amino acids, and the liquid was composed of sugars. There was no question that it was what he said, but the more important question was what he made it with. He had taken twigs earlier that day and turned them into a carbohydrate snack. I jerked a few times before I finally fell asleep.

Avin came by that morning and informed me that two of the council members were there and would be ready to meet me later in the day. He also explained that several of the council members were in the Outer World, as they called it, working on various projects. He also told me that the head scientist, Alder Dimms, was going to speak as well. Apparently, Dr. Dimms was the authority on the hyperdimensional wormhole travel mechanism that had brought me there and did 90 percent of the research that helped them isolate the gene sequence in the human genome. Avin claimed this was a task that scientists of my world had not done.

Avin and I both made our way down a dark hallway toward what looked like a door, but it was much larger. We got to the end of the hall, and the door opened slowly.

"Are you nervous?"

"A little, but I feel pretty good. I slept much better than I thought I would."

"That's good. I was afraid you wouldn't sleep at all."

"Me too. Let me ask you before we arrive. Do you truly trust these men?"

"Yes. I have known them all for a very long time. They have all helped me in one way or another."

"But what if I get any of those feelings when we go before them?"

"You won't. Trust me."

We walked into a small room that only had a few chairs and a table. It wasn't all that fancy, to say the least. I was quite pleased that it wasn't fancy. Maybe the council members were down-to-earth sort of people

"Hello, Seravin. Welcome to you as well, young Oriphate."

This was Dr. Dimms. He was an older gentleman, with brownish grey hair. He wore clothes that resembled those worn by humans on Earth. He had on a brown jacket and slacks. He also had small glasses that seemed to keep sliding down his crooked nose.

"It is such a pleasure to finally mean you, Robert Stevens. I hope your stay here in Aristrasia has been enjoyable so far."

"It has been interesting to say the least."

"Well, sit down; I have a lot to tell you. Avin, if you would."

"Yes, thank you."

"The council members are running a little late as always. I am going to go ahead and start my portion of the presentation. It isn't much of a presentation, though. I haven't had much time to prepare. I had no idea when you would arrive. I was hoping I got you near the castle."

"We landed on the shore, and that was relatively close."

"I knew I should have used the cross-directional vector constant instead of the sigma constant. Wormholes are tricky business."

"I understand."

"As do I."

"Well, let's get to it. Robert, I suppose you know why you are here."

"Yes."

"The energy flux that opened a while back has caused a shift in the time space continuum of our dimension here, and it is our responsibility to keep the Outer World safe and prosperous. Elberion has already suffered at the hands of this equilibrium imbalance. The people of Elberion were a hunter-gatherer type society, and quite hardheaded. I tried to persuade them to leave, but they won't. They were all killed a few days late by a huge storm, comparable to what you think of as a tornado in your reality. We don't really know what opened the flux or why, but I do know one thing for sure. It originates from a black hole."

"A black hole?" Avin asked.

"Yes. This is a star that is in its oldest stage of life. I am currently working on the dynamics of the black hole, but I don't have it yet. I also know that you, Robert, are capable of entering the positive flux, and you will be the first person to complete the sixth trial."

"Are you absolutely sure I can do this?"

"Yes, I am quite sure you will be able to complete it. The only thing I am not sure of is what you will see when you enter."

"What about the Third Dimension? Are these fluxes affecting the balance in my reality?"

"I am not certain about that, but it could possibly be having adverse effects on the Third Dimension."

"Well, what happens after I return from the positive flux?"

"Then you will enter the negative flux, and if my calculations are correct, then the negative flux will cease to be and the black hole responsible for the negative flux."

"What causes the positive flux then?" Avin asked.

"That is a good question, and I am afraid I don't know. I haven't spent as much time studying the positive flux as I have the negative."

"Don't you mean, 'As I have'," a voice said from behind us. At that exact moment I felt a shiver and a cold feeling come over me that was much different than any of the warnings I had got ten in the woods.

"Well, Smirneth. I wasn't expecting to see you here."

Avin turned around with the utmost quickness as if he had been stabbed from behind.

"What are you doing here?"

"He is here on official business, Avin, and we would deeply appreciate your cooperation."

"Smirneth, what business could you possible have here besides..."

"Seravin, hold your tongue. Hello, Oriphate. My name is Fargin, and I am one of the five council members. I have come to introduce you to Smirneth. He has apprehended the man who killed the traveler."

"Yes, I was to meet the traveler at a disclosed location, but he never came. Just so happens that I meet his killer the next day. He seems to be insane."

"Yes, Seravin. We have tried to make sense out of his foolishness, but we cannot shake him."

"So, I thought maybe the great Oriphate could speak to him."

"No, Smirneth. Robert is not ready for that. I would like to see the man first."

"I am afraid that will be impossible," Fargin said in a strange tone.

"Why is that?"

"Smirneth has put an enchantment on the south tower that only he can enter into, but..."

"But what?"

"Well, Seravin, the boy here can enter. His powers are great enough to overcome the spell."

"Smirneth, you have done this on purpose."

"I can't help that your magic is weak."

With that, Avin jumped from his spot and was caught by Dr. Dimms.

"No, Avin, you must calm down."

"Yes, Avin, you must control your temper."

"I don't trust you, Smirneth, and I never will. You betrayed us all."

"Oh, Avin, can't you learn to forgive and forget?"

"Not when someone almost leads me to death."

"That was years ago. I am a changed man. I have seen the error of my ways, and I am here to help you."

"Well, I don't think Robert is ready for this. We should wait until he enters the flux."

"Avin, the man has no powers. The Oriphate has defeated the cursed beast. You said so yourself."

"I just don't think it is a good idea. He cannot control his powers yet."

"All the better," said this man Smirneth in a nasty tone.

Smirneth and the Man in the Tower

Later that afternoon, Avin told me about his past with Smirneth, the Magician of Granate. It seems that Smirneth was a scientist much like Dimms years ago, and he had developed all the techniques for creating magic. Avin also explained that Smirneth used and unsanctioned method for creating his magical powers, and it was much different from the powers that Avin had. It seems that Smirneth was quite the revolutionary in his day, and he didn't always agree with Dimms and the other scientist who worked day and night to discover the secrets of the positive flux.

When the negative flux first opened, Smirneth was well on his way to developing his own form of magic. Avin explained how he did it in great detail, but it was hard to understand. Smirneth had convinced many of the councilmen that his method was much more advanced than the one used to train Avin and his peers, but most of them didn't pay him any attention. Smirneth was most angered by this, and he took several young men and used his technique anyway.

He claimed that this technique would allow his followers to enter the negative flux, and thus destroy it. Well, Smirneth tested this technique on one of Avin's lifelong friends, and it didn't work. The girl that Smirneth used was killed in the flux, and Smirneth was banished from Granate for ten years. Avin believed he should have been killed for his cowardliness, but he was simply banished.

He continued to work on his studies in exile, and soon the ten years were over. Smirneth returned to plead his case to the council, but he had a different case to argue. Smirneth claimed that he had found a way to use the energy of the negative flux to create the most power magic had ever known. Smirneth didn't really believe that, though.

"He didn't discover anything. He just wanted to buy time so he could conduct more studies, but his time is up. He had his little argument, and now he has to realize that the flux has to be destroyed."

"Do you think he would try to stop us from destroying it?"

"No, but I still don't trust him. He has done too many things in the past to lose my trust. He was a ruthless person years ago, and I fear he hasn't changed."

"The council seems to trust him."

"They don't trust him; they fear him and what he can do, because he knows so much about the negative flux. Sometimes I wonder if they even trust me. They don't really care what we do one-way or the other, as long as their regions are safe.

"So they don't really have any power; they just monitor you and Dimms?"

"I don't understand what you mean."

"What I mean is who actually has the power to make decisions?"

"Well, none of us has any power. We just agree to do what is best for the people. We get together, discuss the options, and then do it. No one has absolute authority."

"That seems to be a pretty good system."

"It doesn't always work as well as you would think at first."

"I can understand that; nothing works perfectly all the time. Something else was bothering me, though. I felt the shiver of cold come over me when Smirneth entered."

"That's because he apparated. Anytime a being does that you are going to feel the sign of danger because they appear so fast."

"I think I should speak to the killer, don't you?"

"Yes, but later. You could very well kill him by accident, and we need him alive."

That night we all ate together. The two council members who were there, Dr. Dimms, Avin, Smirneth, and I all sat around a small table. Dimms was speaking to one of the council members about energy conservation, and the other council member was busy asking me about the Third Dimension. Smirneth and Avin were both very quiet, but I would notice that every few seconds they were steadily looking at each other. Soon the silence broke, and Smirneth addressed Avin directly.

"Seravin, do you remember that fateful day on the plain?"

"Yes, Smirneth, I remember it quite well."

Everyone except Dr. Dimms seems to be puzzled by the question.

"Smirneth, why must you bring that up?" Dimms said in a troubled tone.

"I'll tell you why, Doctor," Avin said. "Because Smirneth is an old bitter fool who has to expose every weak moment and every hurtful experience a person has so he can enter his mind and disrupt his brain patterns."

"Now, Avin old boy, why, would I want to do that?"

"Well, maybe so I couldn't read the Oriphates' conscious thought."

"That's enough, Avin," said Heron, the other present councilman. "Smirneth is merely reflecting on the past. Why would..."

"Why would he bring up the day he nearly let me die? I don't know—why would he?"

With that, Avin got up and walked out, leaving his meal half-finished. Dr. Dimms ran after him.

Later, Avin and I sat alone in the tiny domicile. The hour was drawing near, and it would not be long before I would travel into the flux. Dr. Dimms was preparing the time void, as he called it. It was very clear that no one from this reality could get near the flux when activated, so he had to prepare the portal that I was to enter.

Avin sat fuming, still angry about what Smirneth had said. There appeared to be a lot of history between the two of them, and Avin didn't really seem to want to talk about it. The fact that Smirneth had caught the killer angered Avin more than anything.

"He almost destroyed the entire planet with his foolish experiments, and then he just walks back in here with a criminal, and they bring him right in. I swear he is up to something. I must still protest your speaking to that killer until you enter the flux successfully."

I didn't argue with Avin. He knew better than I, and he seemed to have dealt with matters such as this before. More importantly, he had dealt with Smirneth, and he was convinced that Smirneth was trying to cause problems.

"It's not that I think he is trying to stop us from destroying the flux, because he has realized the sure danger of it, with Elberion being destroyed, but I know he has his own interest in mind."

"Please, Avin, I must know before I enter into the flux. Tell me what happened between you two. I must know what kind of person I am dealing with here."

"All right, but it is one of the most serious matters I have ever been involved in."

"I understand fully."

"Well, I was in my eighth year of my magician training, and Argangal was my master, and he always will be. You must understand a little bit about Argangal and his race first. This species of creature was the last of the true magical cardholders in this universe. They were a magnificent group—very noble, very proud. They were winged creatures, with wings much like a bird, I suppose. Their wingspan was quite large, more than ten feet but no longer than twelve. They were fully capable of doing magic, because they were here when the flux first opened. You see, there were many different statues here that were thousands of years old, and they just happened to be one such group. The flux opened, and the statues were brought to life. They could enter the positive flux, and they taught us a lot of what they knew about the flux.

"As soon as the negative flux opened, they warned us of its powers, and the evil group that was responsible for opening it had died as a result. Argangal claimed that even though they were all killed, they were cursed as well. He also claimed to have seen some of them walking the ground. He warned us all to stay away from the flux, but Smirneth would not listen. He believed that Argangal and the others of his group, including me, were trying to prevent him from using the powers held by the flux. He looked at it like a most logical people would, I guess. He thought that the power of the negative flux was comparable to the positive flux.

"Well, he made hundreds of calculations and worked day and night to discover what the flux held. He was also making his new form of magic on the side. Dimms had been watching him closely, but he was preparing the magic in secret. Unluckily, he finished his damned magic first, and without as much as one test, he shot himself with it and became the most powerful person in the inner realm. Are you following all of this?"

"Yes."

"This changed Smirneth. He became more egotistical, and he got extremely spiteful of Dimms and Argangal, he really seemed to hate me, because I was coming along so nicely with my training. He knew I could eventually become as powerful as Argangal, and he couldn't stand the fact that I was from the forest."

"Why is that? What's the big deal about you being from the forest?"

"Well, the only group of people considered lower than the Woodsmen, which I used to be and was very proud to be, are the Elberions."

"Who were killed?"

"Exactly. I will get to that in a moment. Smirneth hated the Elberions even more than the Woodsmen, but he really hated Staluens, like Argangal. He hated the fact that he wasn't the smartest, most powerful being in the inner realm, and he wanted to be. So he started trying to do everything in his power to pull power from Argangal and the other Staluens, and he started drafting children to undergo his magical training."

"But didn't the council try to stop him?"

"That's a good point to bring up. You see, there was no council then, because the Staluens ruled over Aristrasia. After Smirneth murdered one of his students in the negative flux, Argangal stepped in, but Smirneth refused to stop. So, he was arrested, and his students were outraged. One of his most eager students challenged me to fight in the fourth trial for the freedom of Smirneth. Luckily, I managed to win, but the others freed Smirneth, and he killed Argangal out of spite. I did everything I could to stop them, but I wasn't strong enough. Pure luck saved me, or the grace of some higher power, because I was sure I was dead. The Piper showed up on the plain minutes after the battle. Smirneth, the coward, had left me and all my classmates for death.

"The Piper brought me back to life with his flute, but it was too late for anyone else. Argangal died in my arms."

"Avin, I am so sorry."

"No—don't be, Robert. You know as well as I that it was fate. Argangal explained to me as he died that it was the will of fate. I promised him someday that I would avenge him someway, but I haven't yet."

"So the council was appointed then."

"Yes, well you are partly correct. They were not really appointed; they just sort of moved in. The five of them were all governors of the most prominent regions here, and they promised to be fair and work with us. They were all very well respected and highly recommended by the Piper, and Dimms is very good friends with two of them, but they just happen to be two of the ones who are gone. So we all decided to disband all magical research, and Smirneth was exiled. No one really know what happened to his students, but we all have our own explanations—none of which hold water."

"Do you think Smirneth is still messing with the negative flux?"

"It is possible, but he isn't supposed to. I hope he isn't."

"Oh, yes, what about Elberions and all that?"

"Some believed that Smirneth put a curse on the regions he hated, but Dimms has pretty much disproved that with research done on the negative flux. He has connected the destruction of Elberion with the imbalance of the flux, and the math apparently proves it all. Come this time tomorrow, you will be the most powerful creature in this universe, and I believe that this is the thorn in Smirneth's side. He has been the most powerful for many years now, and you threaten his power more than any other person has before."

"He won't try to kill me, will he?"

"He can't. You are already too powerful. Look, you had better sleep awhile before you enter the flux. You need to get some rest."

Surprisingly, I fell asleep quite easily.

In my deep slumber, I began to dream just as I feared I would. Dreams had become somewhat of a fright since the vision. The night before I had dreamed about the young girl, and I feared that I would again. Before I arrived here, my dreams had been generally delightful, but I found that my subconscious mind had changed quite a bit. It seemed as if I didn't really sleep anymore. My dreams had become so real, that it felt like I was awake all the time. The dream I had about the girl the last time I slept was so real that it felt as if I were there at the time. She was alive in the dream, but I knew that was impossible, because I had seen her lying dead on the altar. But, then again, I also saw her jump straight up, giving me the worst scare of my life. I was sure I had lost it, but Avin assured me it was perfectly normal for Oriphates to see things. He explained that it could be symbolic, somewhat of a metaphor for something that was going to happen or did happen.

It scared me so to think that there were people, if you could call them that, capable of doing that to someone, anyone, or anything. I couldn't possibly imagine how that could have happened. I hoped that this vision was symbolic, but symbolic for what? Could it be that someone was going to be killed? I wondered about this deep in a world of unconsciousness. The world of sleep had become a field of wonder—a logical state of deep pondering, if you will. It was much like Sherlock Holmes stories I had enjoyed so much as child, but rather than sitting by the fire with a pipe pondering a mystery, I did the pondering in my sleep. I had never had such intense thought while I was awake, much less while I was asleep.

I sat, or slept rather, with all these thoughts popping up about what the vision meant. I thought carefully about what had happened, who was there, and why it happened, but I kept coming up short. I would soon have my answer, and it wasn't the answer I wanted.

Suddenly, I found myself in a strange place where I had never been before. Slowly, I rose from a dark hole of some sort; I gently floated to the surface and found myself staring into the eyes of a man I didn't know. He sat Indian-style, as my grandfather would say, in the middle of a small, square room. He appeared to be eyeing me, and out of nowhere, he burst into a slight giggle. It was a creepy sort of laugh, much like a clown, but much softer and quite a bit higher. He sat there and laughed for a good twenty seconds, looking off and all around the room haphazardly, and then he stopped suddenly. He quickly turned his attention to me and laughed shortly, and stopped again.

He didn't offer to stand or speak until I moved in closer. First of all, he slivered back a few feet and stood up. He passed to and for, never taking his eyes off of me. All this made me quite nervous, but I was not afraid. I felt as if this man was no threat to me, but I wasn't sure how I knew this. Somehow, I knew he was weak.

"I was hoping you would come and see me before you took your journey," he said as he eyed me quite eagerly. I was very sure I knew well what he was referring to. Naturally, it was a reference to the fifth trial.

"Oh, really," I said quickly after he spoke. "Why is that?"

"I wanted to go ahead and let you know that you are going to fail. You are no Oriphate. Clearly you are just a boy. Those men you put so much trust in and the fools who have brought you here are a bunch of lying quacks."

"And who are you referring to?"

"Well, Smirneth for one, and that idiot Dimms. They are all going to die soon enough, and I will witness it all, and my master will kill you as well."

"Who is your master?"

"I am afraid I cannot tell you that, old friend," he said with a slight giggle. "But I think you will know soon enough."

With that the man walked over to the corner, laughed much louder than he had before, and pulled something from his shirt. I was well enough ready for anything, but what I saw when he turned around wasn't what I was expecting. He pulled out a small doll, looked at it for a moment, and started to laugh once more.

"Don't worry; she won't hurt you, little boy," the man said in a strange voice that clearly wasn't his own. It was a high-pitched voice that sent chills down my spine. The doll was no more than a foot tall, and it didn't appear to have any clothes on. Where he got the doll or why he had it puzzled me, and then it came to me.

"You killed that girl and the traveler. You did it. You're the man Smirneth captured in the woods."

"Bravo, you little fool," the man said. He then screamed out in a low, violent tone and jumped at me. He flew through the air as if he were weightless, and just as fast as he had flown toward me, he flew right into the back wall of the square room with such force that he cracked the wall a bit.

After he managed to get up, he staggered around. Eventually, he found the doll lying near where he had jumped. "It really is him, you really are the…" and with that, I woke up.

It wasn't long after I had woken up, when Avin came into my chambers.

"Good morning, Robert. I hope you slept well." Avin said this in an awkward manner as if he knew I hadn't.

"Well, I did have an interesting vision."

"Yes, I already know about it. It seems that our good friend, Smirneth, went to speak with our prisoner early this morning, and he found him in a different state of mind."

"So it was him. You mean I was really there?"

"Yes, I'm afraid so. It seems that you are more powerful than any of us thought. Dimms made a reasonable guess, and he thinks that you used your subconscious mind to create an absolute likeness of yourself that is fully capable of going anywhere it pleases."

"At the time, of course."

"I'm afraid I don't follow."

"I mean that I can go anywhere at that point in time, rather than say, the future or the past."

"I would suppose you are correct. After all, this did happen last night. But, who knows what will happen, or what powers you will receive after you enter the—"

"Yes, about that. I was hoping I could talk to the prisoner myself before I enter the flux."

"I have already protested this, Robert; I don't think it is a good idea. It is not that I don't think you are capable of defending yourself against him. I am afraid you will kill him."

"Why would I kill him?"

"Not meaning to, of course. You could have killed him last night. Smirneth said he could hardly stand. If you go up there now, you will kill him. Your powers are in you—in your mind, of course—but in your conscious mind you have no control over your subconscious."

"After I enter the flux, will I?"

"Dimms has mapped out every possible aspect of the mathematics, and it shows that you will. Your conscious mind will not exist. It will cease to be, and your subconscious will become your full consciousness. You won't have to sleep, you will know every truth, you will read thoughts and hear things that don't even exist in my mind—anyone's mind. You will become omnificent, and omnipresent. Everything, from the most simple truth to the most complicated fallacy, will become present at your very whim."

This sudden burst of explanation of my soon-to-be state was quite disturbing to me. I wondered why this detailed description had not been elaborated on in the past few days. Avin had walked over to the wall, looking off from me.

"I'm sorry, but Dimms stayed up all night working all of this out. Finishing up his work, he completed his theory last night. He has worked on it for the past ten years, while trying to find you. He is absolutely sure his theory is correct, and when you come back from the flux, it will become his and your greatest accomplishment. Are you ready?"

"Yes."

Robert, the Rocking Chair, and His Rebirth in the Flux

Avin and I walked down several hallways, which were dimly lit with crude torches. It seemed that every hall was the same, and I wondered how a group of men could accomplish such great feats in such a dump, but that question was answered when we reached Dimm's laboratory. It was quite different from any of the other places I had been in the castle. It was well lit with what seemed to be electric lights, and it was full of complicated-looking machinery. It also had boards, or windows rather, that had all sorts of mathematical calculations on them. The formulas stretched the whole length of the room, which was at least a hundred feet. Even some portions of the walls had formulas scribbled on them in quite a few places.

"Good morning, gentlemen," Dimms called out from behind a large machine. "I am glad to see you, Mr. Stevens. Are you ready to embark on the greatest journey of your life?"

"Yes, I suppose."

"Well then, step this way, please."

Dimms took me over to what appeared to be a large hole in the wall. He explained that this "vortex" would take me to the entrance of the flux, and I would enter there.

"It will take a few minutes to warm up completely, but it will not take long. If you and Avin just want to wait in the lounge, I'll come get you when it is ready."

So Avin and I sat in this small room, awaiting the vortex. I was extremely eager, and I know that Avin could tell.

"Are you nervous?"

"Yes, very. I hope Dimms is right."

"Oh, I trust him more than anyone here."

This got me to thinking. I started to question Smirneth and the others. They all seemed shady. I could hardly tell if they were trustworthy. And a question came to mind, and a possible answer to it.

"Avin, I was wondering why Smirneth was so eager for me to see the killer. Do you think it is because he is hiding something?"

"Hiding what?"

"Well, if I could have killed the man, then maybe Smirneth wanted me to kill him."

"That is a very interesting deduction. I swear, you are really turning into quite the Oriphate. I haven't really thought about it like that. I just guessed that he wanted you to get information from him, but I never though about the fact that Smirneth already could know the information that the man has and doesn't want anyone else to find out."

Avin and I sat there for awhile longer, chatting about the flux and Smirneth. It was certainly clear that Avin was ready to act on Smirneth; he just didn't have enough evidence to prove Smirneth had done anything wrong, and for that matter, neither did I. I wasn't even sure if Smirneth had done anything wrong. He just seemed very cunning and sly.

Smirneth was one of those people who stuck out in a crowd of five thousand. He seemed to be looking rather sneaky every time we met, and his curled smile was always accompanied by his bushy eyebrows. He blinked quite a bit as well, and my grandfather always said, "If a man blinks more than five times in one sentence of conversation, then his is dishonest." My grandfather was quite good at judging character. He had worked with the public for so long, he could talk to someone for only a few minutes and tell you whether or not he wanted to do business with him or not, and he was generally right about him.

I was not as good at this as my grandfather, but then again, I was not dealing with a regular person. Smirneth was a powerful magician, and he was capable of so many things I didn't understand. I just hoped I would be able to figure out what Smirneth's true intentions were when I returned from the flux. I was afraid the flux wasn't going to do anything to me or worse, kill me.

Avin and I sat in silence for awhile before Dimms returned for us. He was ready for me to enter the flux. So we walked back down the hallway toward the lab. It was a shaky walk—one that felt like walking into battle or into an old house that was supposed to be haunted. You could say I was scared to death. This was definitely the most frightening walk I had ever taken.

We reached the large, circular entrance, and Dimms walked behind a large machine and quickly started punching buttons and keys.

"Now, Robert, when the vortex opens, just step inside, and you will be right at the flux. There will be a large door that will open once you step out of the vortex. As soon as you walk within a few meters of the door on the other side, it will slide open as well. Then the door on the other side leads to the flux, and you will be sucked into it, so to speak."

"Suck me in? How will I get out?"

"Good question. I am afraid I don't know. You will come back, though, I promise."

This really scared me. He didn't know how I was going to get back. That was a hell of a note.

Avin patted me on the shoulder and nodded. This was to assure me that everything was all right. Dims nodded as well, and the vortex burst open in luminous light and energy that sparkled and burned in such a way that I could hardly be afraid. I took a deep breath and walked toward the vortex. Taking one last look back at Dimms and Avin, I jumped in.

Traveling through the vortex was much like the trip to Aristrasia. It seemed quite similar to the tube of light that I had flown through, but there were a few important differences. It wasn't quite as violent as the trip I had taken previously. It was also much slower. I didn't really know what made it different, but from what Dimms had said, it was the same mechanism.

He described it as "hyperdimensional travel," just as Avin had mentioned before. The hyperdimension was its own dimension, or that was the way I understood it. It was simply a means of traveling between dimensions, much like a highway. It just takes you from one place to another.

The thing I didn't really understand was how it could take me to another place in the same dimension. A lot of these things were extremely hard to understand, and I didn't bother with most of them. It was in my nature, though, to question things, because I was only human, but would I become more than human, like Avin and Dimms had said? Only time would explain this great mystery.

Soon enough, maybe too soon, I stepped through the other side. Well, I suppose I should say I was thrown onto the ground. It wasn't all that painful, though. It was much like being pushed down. The place where I lay was grassy and quite warm. The suns overhead beat down mildly on the back of my neck. I slowly got up and looked around. The vortex had disappeared, and the lush field and rolling hills went on behind me as far as my eyes could see. The place was extremely beautiful. It was quite a change from the dark castle I had been in for several days. It felt good to be outside in the sun, and it almost made me forget why I was there.

I looked over my shoulder and saw the huge metal door. It was at least thirty feet high and twenty feet wide. The tube itself was only about ten feet long, and that confused me. I wondered how the flux could be contained in this short tube. I took another one of those deep breaths and slowly walked toward the large door. The large door began to slide apart, just as Dimms had said. I watched the giant doors slowly slide open. It seemed like hours before they were fully open, and I stepped inside the tube cautiously. As soon as I stepped inside, the large doors shut with great force. They closed a thousand times faster than they had opened, and it was quite loud.

I was a little confused at this time, because nothing was really happening. The large door that led to the flux was very different from the one that had brought me inside. It was very colorful, and it had quite a few drawings on it. It had four or five men painted on it and several women. One of the women was completely naked and she had huge wings, which resembled those you would think of on an angel. The door also had strange writing on it. I wasn't sure how to get in or what to do.

I eventually sat down, because I was at a loss. Dimms had said the doors would open once I got inside, but it had been a good ten minutes and nothing happened. I was beginning to think I was going to be stuck in the tube, and then it happened.

The door didn't as much open as it did break away. I watched every single piece of the door break away and fly into the void of light that lay behind it. At first, it started to crack up the middle. The small crack soon turned into a huge crack, and the door stared to fly into the void. Large pieces of the door started to break away, until the whole door was gone. But I wasn't sucked into the flux as Dimms had said I would be. I just stood there looking into the void. So I decided that I would have to walk into the void. I would have much rather have been pulled in, rather than walking in, but I had to do it. So I slowly walked toward the flux and jumped in quickly.

The flux was quite different inside than I had expected. I found myself flying over what seemed to be mountains. I could see rivers and beautiful waterfalls beneath me. I soared through clouds and over hills. It was a wonderful experience, I must say. As I flew along, I got much closer to the ground. I flew over several huge waterfalls and on along the huge river below me. I once got so close to the river that I could feel the misty waterfall behind me, and I could smell the clean, clear water below me.

I quickly began to go higher, elevating steeply. I soared once again into the sky and through the clouds. The higher I got, the quieter it got. Soon the world below faded from view, as did all the wonderful feelings inside, because I found myself in a strange place. An uneasy feeling came over me as I found myself in a vacant place. It was simply a white area, and I was merely floating about in the area. I guess you could call it a room, but it didn't feel like a room. I don't really know how to describe this place, but it was strange. I floated there in limbo for a moment, when something started flying toward me.

This small object got closer, and I soon realized that it was a chair. It resembled a rocking chair. It looked very much like a rocking chair that sat in my mother's store so many years ago. She had bought it at a flea market with plans to sell it, but no one ever bought it. It sat there until the day my grandfather sold the store, and he decided to bring it home. He often sat in it, as did I.

It flew around me a few times in a circular pattern. I watched it go around me several times, and it soon found its way to where I was floating. In a violent fashion, the chair quickly shot underneath me. I sat in the chair wondering why it was here, and I then found myself tied to the chair with leather straps that appeared from nowhere. I was completely helpless, but I was not scared yet. It seemed to me that the situation could have been worse.

The chair took me along the void. I could tell we were moving, but it was hard to tell where we were going, because everything seemed to look the same. It was just white, and I couldn't tell which way we were moving. I started to get a little uneasy as the chair increased its speed. Before long, we were traveling so fast that I could feel myself being forced against the back of the chair. The only thing that was holding me in the chair were the straps. If it had not been for them, I would have been thrown from the chair.

Suddenly, a figure appeared before me traveling a thousand miles an hour, and the chair came to a complete stop. The figure, who appeared to be an elderly man, was only inches away from me. We were face-to-face, and the man didn't seem to be in a great mood. His facial expression was quite stern, and he looked very angry. Suddenly the chair moved back a few feet, and the man's mouth opened. What came out of his mouth was the loudest noise I had ever heard. It echoed through the void and bounced off every atomic particle present. I felt the sonic burst rush through me like an earthquake. It shook me to the very core. My teeth rattled and clattered as the subsonic waves bounced off my face. It was all the old chair could do to take this sudden pulse of sound energy, but the chair had to have been strong, because it had traveled through the flux with such speed.

The man continued to scream, and the screams got louder and louder. The sound was so incredible. The echoing pulses were growing in size. I could almost see the vibrations illuminating out of the man's mouth. In the blink of an eye, the chair started to spin around and around the man. At first, it started off slowly. I went around him several times, but the chair slowly started to get faster and faster, until I could not even see the man. The chair was going so fast that I could hardly breathe. It would seem that this would have killed me, but for some reason it didn't. I continued to spin around and around the man.

The chair soon stopped spinning around the man, but the man was gone when I stopped spinning. It took the chair several minutes to stop, and it took even longer for the sounds to stop. Once the sounds stopped, I found myself alone, strapped to the chair. When every last sound had faded into the flux, the chair shot straight into the air above. Going even faster than before, the chair traveled faster than the light into the never-ending void of the flux. I looked above, and all I could see was the never-ending laminating whiteness of the void, increasing in every way, and soon the white faded away, and the multitude of colors and bright flashes overtook my psyche. The spectrum of electromagnetic waves rushed over me, recreating my thoughts. I felt my brain burn inside my head. Every neuron and synapse was bombarded with the rushing sodium that filtered through the channels, and polarization of cell membranes had reached it maximum level. Action potentials fired throughout my body, and every muscle began to contract. The violent shakes created pulses through me, jerking me from side to side, up and down, through, between, over, under and out. Inside my cranium lay my neural tissue, flowing like waves on the ocean. I could see my brain, melting onto the surface, working its melody and beating to the destruction of itself.

My brain then recreated itself much like the phoenix, as it burst into flames. Born again from the ashes, my brain reconstructed itself from front to back. I watched atomic particles form complex polymers before my very own eyes. As they came together, I saw the formation of my cerebrum, which led to the formation of the cerebellum. The medulla soon formed, and the spine took shape before my eyes. Dazzling before me were organs that came together in such a vibrant fashion. I watched my digestive system construct itself before me, and my eyes soon came about, protruding from the nerves formed. Nerves of all sorts shot from my spinal cord and down as far as five feet.

Next came the cardiovascular system. By this time I was watching this from the shell being created, and I saw my old self-fading away in the distance. Arteries and veins of all sizes shot from my newly constructed heart that soon started pumping blood as it would inside your body. I felt the power rushing through my blood. It was an intoxicating feeling that I could hardly stand. It felt wonderful. Before long my musculature had been formed; my skin followed suit. I was standing naked and reborn.

In the mix of color and light came a voice from somewhere far away.

"Oriphate, you have come from a long distance, and your help is greatly appreciated. You have been recreated in the likeness of yourself, and your powers are strong. You must now return to Aristrasia and complete your task, destroy the evil that plagues their world, and the power that will potentially destroy yours. Good luck, Oriphate."

Then it was almost like the bottom fell out from underneath me. I was falling fast down into the void and out of the colors. I eventually found myself falling back into the white zone. By this time I was going extremely fast, and afraid I would never stop falling, until an old friend caught me. It was the rocking chair. As soon as it caught me, it did what it did best. We flew through the air faster than ever. When the chair stopped this time, I wasn't strapped in, and I went flying through the flux. I had to have been going fast enough to break the sound barrier. Then there was a loud boom and a blinding flash.

I woke lying on the cold ground. It appeared to be grass, but it was dark wherever I was. I slowly started to walk toward what looked like lights in the distance. Once I got closer, I realized it was the castle. I noticed a small figure standing out front. It was Smirneth, awaiting my return, no doubt.

I walked back toward the castle through the wet grass. The fresh dew glistened in the moonlight, and the sweet smell of flowers filled the morning air. It looked as if the day was going to be pleasant, and I was quite happy to have made it out of the flux successfully.

The Tower Revisited

Smirneth came into focus as I drew closer to the castle. He was wearing that same old stupid smile he always did, and he seemed quite happy to see me. I could tell by the expression on his face that he had seen me, but I wasn't sure why he was awaiting my return. I figured Avin would have been out, but how would he have known? That raised a more important question: How did Smirneth know?

"Good morning, boy. Was your little trip good?"

I looked as Smirneth, and he looked at me. I suppose he didn't get a good look at me until that moment, because I saw the expression on his face change rather quickly. His eyes got wide, and his mouth dropped open. For once, he seemed to be at a loss for words. He stuttered a bit and turned away. "You can hear the voice; he heard it." Smirneth said this a few times to himself, and then he addressed me directly.

"You heard the voice, didn't you?"

"Yes, Smirneth, I heard a voice, but I am not sure whose voice it was."

"You fool; it was the voice of Argangal, the stupid creature Avin told you of. His soul is trapped in the positive flux. That is how I trapped him, with a spell. You heard him?"

"Yes, Smirneth, I heard his voice, and I was rebuilt. My entire body was reconstructed in the flux. I am more powerful now than you can possibly imagine."

"Oh, come off it, you little..." and with that Smirneth shot what seemed to be a ball of blue fire at me. We were about five feet from each other, and the ball of fire came quite quickly, but it passed right through me. It went off, flying toward the woods, and eventually smacked into a tree. The large tree burst into flames and there was a great blue explosion. Smirneth looked as if he could have died.

"Impossible! You couldn't have."

Avin and several of the council members came running out of the castle a few second later.

"What in the devil is going on?" said Avin loudly, and then he noticed I was standing there. "Robert, you are back." He ran over and hugged me. He seemed to be happier than Smirneth was at the moment. The council members were busy scolding him for the destructive fire he had caused.

"Come, let's take a walk."

Avin and I walked along the side of the castle.

"Now, you must tell me what happened."

"Well, it was surreal. I was pulled into a zone of whiteness, and then there were all these colors. I then watched my entire body reconstruct itself from nothing. Then I heard a voice that told me I was to go into the negative flux as soon as possible. He said I would be able to destroy it if I went into it."

"Very interesting. We have a little problem with the negative, but it isn't anything you can't handle."

"What do you mean?"

"Smirneth went and scouted the area around the flux yesterday with Dimms, and they barely made it back. Dimms is conscious right now, but he was out for awhile. It seems that someone is there guarding the flux entrance."

"Well, let's go get them. I feel that I could take on anything right now."

"No, we have to know what we are dealing with first."

"But doesn't Smirneth know what it was? He did go there, didn't he?"

"Yes, but he had no idea what the creatures were that he had to fight off. They blindsided him and Dimms and almost killed them both."

"Speaking of killing, Smirneth tried to kill me earlier."

"Oh, he couldn't kill you if he wanted to. He was testing to see if you were really the Oriphate. He still hasn't accepted it yet, and he never will. To hell with him."

"So what do we need to do next?"

"You are going to talk to the killer. You're going to have to get in his mind and figure out exactly what he was planning to do and why he killed the traveler."

"All right."

Smirneth and I made our way down the dimly lit hallway. I remembered Smirneth saying that only he could withstand the magic that guarded the prisoner, so only he could take me to where the prisoner was being held. It was a little uncomfortable, I must say, walking along with a man who had tried to kill me a few hours ago. But I wasn't afraid of Smirneth, because I knew as well as he did that none of his magic could touch me.

I still didn't really trust Smirneth. He seemed extremely shady, and his motives were distorted. I didn't really understand what he had to gain from all this. Avin had explained to me earlier that Smirneth wanted to do more studies on the negative flux, so why would he want me to destroy it?

Another important question was why did Smirneth capture this man I was about to speak to. Why the hell did Smirneth care that this man had killed the traveler, and what was the traveler's business with Smirneth? It was all very confusing at the time, but I hoped that the prisoner could shed some light on the situation.

Another thing that bothered me was the creatures at the negative flux. How could they have defeated the most powerful magic in the universe? Smirneth seemed quite hurt by the incident. I think his mental state was hurt most by the interaction. If he had defeated Argangal, how could some magical creatures have defeated him?

"Smirneth, I have a question."

"What is it?"

"What were the creatures at the flux?"

"It was like nothing I have ever studied or encountered. They were huge things with red glowing eyes. They attacked me and Dimms. They came out of nowhere. It all happened so fast."

"Do you think the prisoner knows what they are?"

"Well, you're fixing to find out," he said, as we came upon a large opening. The opening led into what seemed to be a deep corridor. It appeared to be bottomless, but I knew that couldn't be true.

"He is at the top of this well in a small room. I'm sure you will recognize it when you get up there."

"Yes, but how do I get up there?"

"Well, boy, that's quite simple. YOU FLY!"

Smirneth swiftly shoved me into the hole, and I started to fall. I watched the sides of the dirty hole go by as I plummeted into the abyss. I could soon hear the water gushing below, and without a sudden notice or warning of any kind, I stopped in mid-air, directly above the underground river. It was quite a well—much different from the underground springs in Iowa.

I was amazed to see that I could fly. It was the strangest feeling I had ever had, and it felt much different from anything that had happened in the flux. This seemed much more real. I slowly floated up the well and past Smirneth, who was sitting on the floor. He watched me rise up past the passage with the same old stupid look on his face. I drifted up toward the top. I could see a small glimmer of light coming from the room that held the prisoner. I was eager to see this character again, and this time was going to be a lot different.

I slowly drifted into the room to see the prisoner sitting in the corner. He appeared to have been crying. He seemed to be in a much different mental state. He soon noticed that I was there, and he seemed frightened at first.

"It's…it's you—you are the Oriphate. Please spare me, I didn't mean to kill them. They made me do it."

"I am not here to kill you. I need information about the killing."

"I can't tell you. They'll know; they always know. You don't understand what you're dealing with. You are meddling with what you can't understand—that I don't understand."

"Why did you kill the girl?"

"Because they made me. I had no choice."

"Who made you? Tell me!"

"I don't know."

"Goddamn it, tell me!"

The man then stood up and came near me. I could feel remorse in the man's steps as he sobbed quietly to himself.

"It was like I was under some sort of spell. I couldn't control myself. I killed the other girls before I finally found her." After saying this, he lifted up the tiny doll that he had presented during our first encounter.

"Believe me when I first saw her I didn't mean to kill her—not like that. It was cold that night. It still frightens me to the bone thinking about it."

I soon found myself watching the actions unfold like pictures in a book. The young girl, probably no older than fifteen, stood outside of a small shelter, watching what appeared to be a group of boys playing some sort of game. She seemed to be enjoying the game quite a bit. She sat and watched in silence, and she soon drifted off behind the small shelter and started to laugh to herself. She seemed very happy.

She wondered along and off in the woods behind, and the feelings of happiness soon disappeared along with the smile on the girl's face. I could feel fear overtake her as she slowly made her way back toward the shelter. Soon, she had produced the doll from insider her baggy dress, and a slight chill seemed to be coming over me. I could tell something wasn't right.

Suddenly the man appeared behind her, but she never saw him. He silently slipped up behind her and slit her throat. She fell to the ground, unable to speak as the blood gushed from the wound. It was long before she had become motionless. She twitched a few times and slowly died. It was a terrible thing to witness. Then the man formed the most unnatural, heinous act you could possible imagine. He took out a small spoon and proceeded with some sort of ritual. Then he removed both her eyes.

I had to turn away and found myself in a completely different place. I was in the woods. Suddenly, a man passed me. It was the traveler. He walked a few feet, and the killer jumped out in front of him. They exchanged words as they slowly passed and circled each other. It wasn't long until the killer produced a small knife and jumped the man. They struggled a few moments, and soon the traveler was dead. The killer rumbled through the traveler's possessions and removed a small parcel from the man's bag. He quickly got all of the man's possessions, cleaned out his pockets, and disappeared into the forest.

Suddenly, it was like I had been fast-forwarded to the future, but I was in the same place. The next thing that happened was quite strange, and it revealed something that was an essential clue to the whole mystery. Smirneth came walking up the area where the man had been murdered. He scoped out the situation, and he seemed quite startled. He looked around the body, noticing that the man had absolutely nothing with or on him. Smirneth paced around a few times, mumbling to himself, "Where is the stone, where is it?" Smirneth was obviously referring to the parcel that the killer had stolen.

I soon realized that Smirneth had a lot more to do with all this than he had told the council, or Avin for that matter. Smirneth ran off quickly, and he was gone into the forest, fast on the trail of the killer. It was almost like he knew which way the killer went, and he was off.

After fast-forwarding once again, I found myself watching the showdown between the killer and Smirneth. Smirneth had him cornered against a large rock wall, and the man had a crazy look in his eyes. The killer pulled out the knife he had used on the traveler, but Smirneth quickly disarmed him. Smirneth grabbed the man with great force and pushed him against the rock wall.

"Where is the stone, you coward?"

"I didn't have it. My master has it."

"You have no master, you little fool. Where is it?"

"I don't have it, old man!"

"Trust me, it will be found, and you will be killed for the mess you have caused. Do you realize we could have stopped all this by now?"

"It matters not, for my master will become powerful—so powerful that you will not be able to stop him."

"To hell, you say. Your so-called master will be found."

With that, I found myself back in the room with the killer. He was sitting in the floor, with his head between his legs, crying his eyes out.

"You see, my master made me do it. I never would have done it. I swear. I must do it. I don't deserve to live."

"Wait—no—who is your master? I must know."

"I have shown you all I can."

Then the man walked over the edge. He dropped the doll into the well and followed suite. I ran over to the edge and watched him fall deeper and deeper, until I could no longer see him.

I floated back down toward the bottom with all sorts of questions in my head. I had quite a few for Smirneth. He was still sitting in the same place as before, smiling that little devilish smile of his.

"Well, that certainly took long enough. For the Oriphate, you are quite slow."

"Cut it, Smirneth. I saw some things up there that involved you, buddy."

"Oh, really. You don't say."

"Yes, I do say. What's the deal with the stone? Why is it so important, and why would this man kill for it and then kill himself?"

"I guess we need to have a little chat about it."

"Well, start chatting."

"All right. You know why you are here?"

"Yes, to stop the flux from destroying our dimension."

"Yes, well you see, the stone you referred to is a magical stone that Dimms and I created years ago. We created it to draw power from the positive flux, but the negative flux opened soon after we created the stone. Dimms wanted to use the stone to destroy the flux, and he warned that the disequilibrium would get worse. Well, I didn't want to destroy the flux. I felt that we could conduct a few studies on it first. I thought we had plenty of time. Well, I kept putting it off, and in the meantime the stone went missing. Dimms blamed me, of course, as did Avin, so it became my responsibility to find it. When I discovered that the traveler had found it, I knew I had to get it from him, but the killer beat me to him. I had spent ten years looking for that damn thing, and I almost had it."

"Why can't you just make another one?"

"We don't have enough time to create another one. It took us fifteen years to build that one."

"Well, I can stop the flux now, so it doesn't really matter. What is more important is why this 'master' would steal it."

"Master, what master?"

"The killer spoke of his master."

"Oh, dear, then someone is planning to use the stone."

"Use it for what?"

"Something evil. We must call the council together."

The Orphiate Constant

A few hours later, we were all gathered together in the main chamber. The two council members were there, Avin, Smirneth, and me, of course. I wondered why the other three council members didn't find it necessary to attend, but I suppose they were busy. It was strange, though. Avin had told me they were merely figureheads, and they didn't really make most of the decisions. He also told me that one of the missing council members had been against bringing me to Aristrasia.

We all spoke to each other as we awaited the arrival of Dimms. Avin and the council members were very interested in what the prisoner had told me. Avin stood and shook his head as I told every last detail. The council members looked very concerned.

"Smirneth," Fargin said angrily, "why didn't you tell us that damn stone was involved? Avin, did you know this? Did the Piper know this?"

"No, I didn't. The traveler, whoever he was, must not have found it necessary to tell the Piper either."

"Really, Smirneth, how could you?"

"I wasn't the only one who knew!" Smirneth said loudly.

At that time, Dimms walked in holding several books and a parchment. The parchment looked quite old, as did the books.

"Afternoon everyone. I see you are all up in arms, and I am quite sorry Smirneth and I didn't tell you about the stone, but for security purposes, we felt…"

"Felt what?" Fargin said. "That we were not to be trusted?"

"No, it is not that," Smirneth said.

"Oh, really, well if you can't trust us, then why the hell are we here?"

"Well," Dimms said loudly, "Three of you are not HERE!"

It was the first time I had heard Dimms raise his voice. He seemed quite angry, and he had brought up a wonderful point.

"Smirneth and I almost died yesterday, and if it hadn't been for him, I would have died. Avin brought the Oriphate here, and I am trying my damndest to save your regions, so please. Now, if you will all kindly sit down, I will try to explain the significance of the stone and the danger it poses."

We all sat down as Dimms set up what seemed to be materials he was going to use to do a demonstration. He got out several small pieces of equipment and pinned the parchment to the wall. It all looked very interesting.

"I think I'm ready. All right, when Smirneth and I started this project, we hadn't even thought of going to the Third Dimension, or the threat of another flux. We just simply wanted to see if more energy could be drawn from the flux in a controlled way. So, we analyzed the energy source from the flux and discovered a strange atomic particle. It was an atom that had four negatively charged particles in orbit around it. We soon realized that we could balance the negative charge with four more electrons. So, logically we figured that it was 2n, or two times the amount of particles in the shell.

"We were quite wrong. We discovered this when we added six particles to oxygen, which has six. Strangely, it only took two of the particles, and it seemed that all the particles that only had eight particles only took enough to get eight. We used this as the basis of the whole study. Taking the particles from the flux, and some we made synthetically, we started constructing molecules.

"As the study progressed, we found that we could construct many different kinds of molecules, and we learned that we could lower the activation energy by conformational changes in molecular structure."

"I'm sorry, Dimms," Avin said very politely, "I don't understand what you are talking about."

"He means that they created enzymes or catalysts. It speeds up chemical reactions."

I was extremely shocked because those words had come out of my mouth. Everyone looked at me strangely.

"Right—Robert, uhh…All right, back to it then. We had several different kinds of chemicals. One that was very interesting was a polymer of carbon that was sweet tasting, and that was glycogen, the chemical that Avin learned to make magically. Another very interesting chemical, which served as the basis for our enzymes, was amino acid sequences. We found out that one conformational change in the structure of the protein could completely change its entire function. It was all very fascinating.

"But that most interesting molecule we created was the nucleic acid polymer. It was by far the most complicated of all the molecules, and it was composed of a sugar backbone and base pairs that was bonded to the sugars and each other. This molecule also seemed to replicate in the presence of several of your enzymes.

"We soon realized that this molecule was the genetic code for all living organisms in the Third Dimension. The one we created contained several base pair sequences that seemed to appear in patterns. These patterns were always the same, and by using several mathematical theorems that Smirneth published, we were able to decipher the code in several hours, and we used this to create a sequence that could draw more energy from the flux.

I spoke up. "You mean you mapped out the entire genetic code."

"Well, no, we just simply figured out the codes we needed to draw the energy. We could have, but it would be useless to do so."

"Do you have any idea how important that would be in the Third Dimension? Wow, I mean you have figured out so much that scientists there are barely even touching on."

"Well, we do have magic."

"Yeah, but the same rules apply, don't they?"

"Not really. You see, in the Third Dimension, scientists believe that the genetic material is just another random process that governs evolution, and it does there. You see, traits, or genes in the deoxyribonucleic acid sequence, are passed on through intercourse in your reality, but here it is just merely a cod, a puzzle, because our world—reality you might say—doesn't work on the same principles that govern yours. The genetic code is a part of a greater design that went wrong somehow in the Third Dimension through their own principles that govern its processes. Your reality is so random that its own processes can't even keep up."

"Why, though? What makes your reality so structured?"

"It is quite complicated, but it all falls back on the same techniques we used to deduce the code. The physical structure of our world—it arrangement, its attributes—all contribute to the processes, from every little microorganism to the stars in the sky. Your dimension is in disarray for some reason, and it has been for billions of years. That is what has allowed such a wide array of organisms and life forms to spring up in just a few million years.

"Is that bad?" I asked.

"No, that is wonderful. That is what allows such a large amount of energy to come here. This place was a wasteland until the flux opened and brought life back to the reality. Everything here was dying, and your dimension saved it. The randomness of your reality is what makes it flourish, and we were just trying to recreate that."

"Well, Dimms," Fargin said, "what of this parchment? What does it mean?"

"I will get to that in a minute. Now, me and Smirneth had the parts of the code we needed, so we set up a lope reconstruction mechanism with a special enzyme that could reconstruct the polymers over and over.

"Not long after we finished the stone, as you all call it, the negative flux opened and the stone went missing. I believed that the stone could correct the problem, but Smirneth, as he usually does, disagreed with me. I seriously though that one of the sequences would disrupt the flux, and it is that sequence that you, Robert, contain on your thirteenth chromosome. It is a useless base sequence in your reality, but it allows for your powers here. The parchment on the wall is the sequence, all mapped out. When decoded, it gives a very interesting value that pointed us to your exact location, your age, sex, and everything else about you. That is how we found you."

"Am I the only one, like Avin said?"

"Yes, it seems that this code contains a lethal recessive trait that encodes for a protein that causes natural abortion in your species, but you survived it. You are part of the greater design, you see. The randomness allowed that gene to be inactive."

"How is that the greater design?"

"You see, the fact the lethal gene is inactive on your chromosome allows for the organization necessary. It allows you to be the Oriphate. The word Oriphate is an essential part of the equation that Smirneth used to construct the sequence that exists in the stone. It is the Oriphate constant that helped us deduce the sequence."

"Well," Avin said, "I guess you could say that chaos has brought order."

"Yes," Smirneth explained further, "it is a paradox. The fact that chaos brought the sequence is what troubled me. From random chaos we achieved a sequence of base pairs that was, in essence, the whole situation to the grand design that Dimms spoke of. It is this sequence that can bring order to the random cause-and-effect-type system of organization that exists in the Third Dimension. But here, it will simply disrupt the negative flux."

"So me living in the Third Dimension does not stop the randomness."

"Right, and that is mainly what Dimms and I disagreed about. The calculations suggested that the amount of chaos in the Third Dimension far outweigh the sequence, but Dimms thinks that it is simply a matter of your biology structure."

"Yes, because this sequence serves no purpose in your reality; therefore, it has no functional value. Structure and function are essential in your reality, but not so necessary here, because we can alter our own reality with energy from yours. That is why you are so powerful here, as is the stone, because by having them, we have disrupted the time space continuum. Neither you nor the stone are supposed to be here, but the disorder you pose—that is, your functional structures, as well as the sequence—will bring order once more."

"This is very hard to understand, Dimms," said Fargin, "and quite frankly, I don't see how it has helped us. The stone has been missing for years. No one has ever used it for a damn thing. If you two could have stopped the flux with it, why didn't you?"

"Because Smirneth thought we could learn from the flux, and I hoped we could as well. We should have just trusted the math and went ahead with it."

"And let it be known," said Smirneth, "that we were going to do it, but the stone was stolen only days before. I spent years looking for it, but never found it, and now I fear that someone is doing something with it, because they know the Oriphate is here to destroy it."

"What could they possibly do?" Avin asked.

"Well, you see, the sequence in the stone is remarkable, and they have the power to draw as much energy from the flux as they can and do whatever they want with it. In other words, they could completely drain the Third Dimension of all its energy."

"No, we can't let that happen. We have to go now. We have to do this now."

"Hold on, Robert. Who would possibly know how to do this? It would be very complicated."

"Yes, but there are other ways to do it without science."

"Yes, with black magic of some sort. We do need to do this and get it over with, as quickly as possible."

I sat there alone in that same old stupid room that I always sat in, waiting. Avin had said it would be best if I got some rest before we started the journey. I was quite excited, to say the least. I was ready to end all of this and see exactly what the hell was going on. I had been told so many things, I was not sure what to believe.

Dimms made a good case, and he seemed to be quite intelligent. He also made Smirneth look like less of a bad guy. Smirneth was much like any scientist. He was just curious about the flux, but some of the things he did with it, from my understanding, were not exactly ethical. But was science really ethical anyway? Ethics and morals didn't really seem to apply to science, but hurting someone or something for any reason was and always will be wrong. Smirneth seemed to mean well, though, and he was going to lead me and Avin to the flux.

Smirneth was up in arms about this whole ordeal. I think he blamed himself for the whole incident, and the council most definitely did. As for Avin, I wasn't really sure. It seems as if Avin blamed himself as much as Smirneth, or anyone else for that matter. It wasn't really anyone's fault, though, because things happen that are out of our control, and that was something this group of people were not used to. They had been using magic to control most everything before all of this happened, and this incident was far out of the reach of any magic, besides the stone.

I understand completely how they all felt. When my mother became ill, I felt like I had lost control myself. Even though I was fourteen years old, I felt like it was my responsibility to correct the problem when, in all actuality, there was nothing I could do about it anyway. I felt helpless—like there was no point in trying anymore—and I soon realized that I had to suck it up and try my best. I couldn't let it get me down, because my mother wouldn't want that. She would want me to be strong and try my damndest to carry on.

This was most definitely my chance to prove myself. This time I had the power to save the entire planet Earth and millions of people in the universe. I didn't feel helpless anymore, and I was sure that my mother would have been proud. I was ready for anything to prove myself, and most of all, to get it all over with and get back where I belonged.

Avin came for me a few minutes later, and we were off. Dimms had readied the dimensional void, and it was time for the showdown. I was more than ready.

The Surprise at the Negative Flux

The three of us walked slowly up the densely grown path. You could tell from the journey up through there the that path had not been used for several years. Smirneth was the only one who knew where we were, because Avin had never been to the negative flux, and this was an alternate path that Smirneth used during his studies on the negative flux. These studies had not been sanctioned by the magical authority that Avin used to serve on, before the council of Granate had taken over the Inner World.

I had been monitoring Smirneth's brain wave activity in order to understand whether he was sincere and loyal to us. Avin had not instructed me to do this, but I found it necessary, because Smirneth's behavior was quite different. He didn't seem to be as cocky as he usually was. He was very serious and extremely somber about the whole ordeal, and he seemed disturbed.

This was a good sign, because it showed that he was legitimate in his quest. His brain wave function seemed to be normal, but they were moving rapidly, which meant he was alarmed. I think we all were a little alarmed, but Smirneth seemed to be the worst, because he had seen what we were going to be against and had almost died at the flux the day before, or so he says.

There were multiple reasons for his concern, and the fact that he had fought the creatures at the flux was only a small part of it. Dimms had described the creatures, and from what he said, Smirneth had saved his life, but Smirneth blamed himself for what was going on here. He finally realized that this could have been taken care of years ago, but his stubbornness had prevented the solution.

Smirneth also knew what the stone was truly capable of, and I think he feared that the most. None of us were sure if the stone had anything to do with the flux, but it was pretty obvious that it did. There was a sense of insecurity about what was going to happen to us that afternoon, and the stone had to be part of it. From Smirneth's brain waves, it was almost certain that he felt the same way. Smirneth's extreme concern made it hard for me to monitor his brain waves, because it was hard to tell exactly what he was concerned about.

The powers that I received in the flux were the most amazing thing I had ever experienced. I wasn't quite as powerful as Dimms had thought I would be, but I was still amazed. Every now and then I would see infrared images in front of us. I was almost as if my brain could tell when a warm-blooded organism was near the path, and the infrared would kick in as soon as the organism came into a specific range.

I could also move objects with my mind. Telepathy was something that always interested me, and I now I could virtually move anything, no matter how heavy it was, with my mind. As I walked along, I would break branches and move small limbs out of the way with merely a thought. My telepathic powers were so strong that I could actually lift myself. That was how I was able to ascend to the top of the tower where the prisoner was held. I could fly as high as I wanted, because my lung capacity was extremely strong, and I could hover over the ground as long as I wanted.

Dimms had explained that my brain was responsible for all my powers, and it was what fueled me. I didn't have to eat anymore, because my brain had developed a mechanism in which ATP was created from the air I inhaled nutrients, as opposed to having to absorb it in my digestive track. It seems that now my digestive system had become some sort of air-filled sac that worked much like a flotation device that aided in flight. All my senses were as much as a thousand times stronger, and my cognitive processes had increased a hundredfold.

My subconscious mind had taken over my body, and my consciousness had been shut down. The reason I knew this was certain, just as Avin had said, was because I didn't feel the need to sleep anymore. Dimms also told me that this was the key to all my powers, because my whole brain functioned as opposed to only two percent of it. It seems that the subconscious mind reveals all truth, and I was seeing things clearly for the first time in my life. It was a great feeling.

Out of nowhere, I felt a strong change in Smirneth's nervous system function. His sympathetic nervous system had increased his heart rate, and his digestive system had slowed down considerably.

"Stop. There is something up there," he said quietly.

Avin looked cautiously and replied, "I don't see anything. Robert, do you?"

"Well, I think there is something, but I don't think it means any threat. It appears to be some kind of animal."

"You're probably right," Smirneth replied. "I'm just a little jumpy. We are almost there. About a hundred yards or so, and we'll be right at the back entrance. It is small hole that we can take to the upper part of the compound. I hope the element of surprise will be on our side."

We walked for another minute or so and soon came upon a large brick building that appeared to be a few stories high. Some parts of the building were quite taller, and the flux entrance was quite high, towering over the rest of the building.

Smirneth led Avin and me into the small hole. We made our way through the tunnel, and it was extremely dark. We eventually found ourselves in a small room that lead into a narrow hallway. There were at least two inches of water on the floor, and the ceiling was steadily dripping in many different places. A multitude of pipes ran overhead.

"All right, you two, we're going up. Have your weapons ready and no heroics," Smirneth said looking deadpan at Avin. "If we are going to get to the flux, we have to work together, and I think it would be best if we stayed together at all times. One more thing—be careful to watch for those yellow pipes. They are full of gas, and if one of them gets hit, we are all gone."

Once we had reached the top of the steps, it soon became clear that we were soon to be discovered. Over thirty strange-looking creatures paced to and fro in every direction. Upon further inspection, I soon realized that they were the creatures I had seen in my first vision. They had performed the ritual on the girl.

It wasn't long before a scruffy-looking elderly man appeared among the creatures. He walked between them, speaking to them as if they were pets of some sort. He called them things like "precious" and "sweetie" as he walked among them. In turn, they seemed quite drawn to him. It was clear that he controlled these freakish-looking monsters.

The monsters themselves were quite interesting without their hoods and cloaks. They appeared to have a face much like a dog, with red, glowing eyes. Their teeth were long and crooked, but they looked more like the teeth of a lizard. All the teeth were quite small and pointy, and occasionally they would lick at their horrid faces with their long, wet tongues. Their skin seemed to be scaly, with patches of fur in various places. Every once in awhile, a fight would break out among them, and they were quite capable of standing erect or on all fours.

"What is that man saying to them?" Avin asked as we hid in the shadows at the top of the stairwell.

"I have no idea," Smirneth replied.

"He's just speaking to the monsters, like pets or something."

"You mean you can understand them?" Avin said in a surprised tone.

"Yes, can't you?"

They both shook their heads in a horizontal direction.

We watched for a few minutes more, hesitant to attack. There didn't really seem to be a window of opportunity, and Smirneth soon gave us the signal. Avin preceded and climbed the wall as Smirneth had instructed him earlier. He was to climb up above the creatures in order to take some of them out before Smirneth and I attacked, because he was most definitely the best shot. As soon as Avin got to his post, the man discovered me and Smirneth, lurking in the shadows.

"Well, look, my children. We have visitors."

Of course, Smirneth was clueless as to what the man had said, and he made a not-so-obvious gesture telling Avin to hold back.

"Welcome to our master's home."

I quickly stepped out.

"This isn't anyone's home. You're all trespassing on sanctioned grounds."

"Oh, I believe you will soon enough discover that we have full right to be here."

"I don't think so, buddy. Why don't you tell your master that the Oriphate has come to put an end to this foolishness?"

"My dear boy, you're the Oriphate? Good, good—the master has been expecting you for some time now. He awaits you as we speak."

I knew that both Smirneth and Avin were oblivious to the content of the conversation, because even I could tell now that I wasn't speaking English anymore. Matter of fact, I realized that I had not been speaking English since I arrived Aristrasia. I could translate their language in my mind and speak it as well.

"What is your business here, old man?"

"OUR business here is to serve our master. Kill the other one and take the Oriphate alive!"

The creatures quickly went into a defensive position, displaying their dominance and posing their attack.

With that, a sonic burst of light shot from afar, taking out several of the creatures. Smirneth and I quickly sprang to action, as Avin continued to fire down on the creatures.

After doing several flips through the air, I landed in the midst of the creatures. I quickly drew my half-staff and fired upon two attacking creatures. I managed to knock them off their feet and flat on their backs, as another charging beast ran straight for me. I swiftly shot into the air and fired below.

As I elevated toward the ceiling, I saw Smirneth holding his own among several of the beasts. Avin was busy firing on a group of them and was slowly being backed into a wall. He soon realized his predicament and jumped against the wall, slowly creeping out of the creatures' reach.

I vigorously shot toward the group and fired an enormous blast right in the middle of the brutes. They went flying off in different directions. I landed not far from the wall. Some of the beasts lay dead on the floor, and some merely stunned.

"Good work," Avin said, joining me below. "Come, we must help Smirneth."

We were both eyeing him, and aggressively shot into the ceiling to be met by an unfortunate blast that sent us flying through the room in opposite directions. It had come from the old man. I viewed him from the corner of my eye as I quickly got to my feet. He laughed heartily at my predicament.

I rapidly fired off several shots with my half-staff. I watched the shots barrel toward him. Two of them traveled parallel to one another, and one strayed off. These three were, without a doubt, the strongest I had ever produced. The stray eventually made its way to where Smirneth was busy fighting. This ball of bright blue fire hit directly behind the mob, killing several of the beasts and knocking others into the air and against the wall behind Smirneth.

The two balls that had been traveling parallel quickly made their way toward the man, and one of them went right through him. Both balls eventually hit the back wall with great force. I soon realized that the wall was about to fall, and Smirneth was right in the midst of it.

"Smirneth!" I screamed out, but soon found myself in the air, flying into the back of the room. The electrical blast was very intense. I slammed against the back wall and fell to the floor. I got up much slower this time, because the blast had weakened me quite a bit, not to mention crashing into the wall. I was able to see that Smirneth was all right, and Avin had joined him.

I was also joined by the old man.

"Well, boy, what did you think of that?" he asked as I drew my wand.

"That won't help you, boy," he exclaimed, and I felt the wand's flight from my hands.

"I don't understand."

"Of course you don't," said the figure as he hovered above me.

"I am the last of the dying religion. My practice has been shunned for thousands of years, but it is a very powerful sort of magic that you cannot feel, hear, taste, or comprehend—black magic."

"So you freaks are the ones who opened this flux with your sick rituals."

"Yes. I was the only survivor, but I stayed here in the shadows, hiding from the world, awaiting deliverance, praying for a savior, and I soon found him, or rather he found me. He gave me power again and hope for my lost brothers and sisters who died here trying to accomplish so many years ago what will be finished here today. They will all rise again as will I."

"To hell you will," I said quickly.

"Don't you see, boy? You can't destroy me. I am impenetrable and resistant to your white magic."

"Why is that?"

"Because the evil things I have done to acquire mine far outweigh the diligence of your magic and the noble way you acquired it. You, boy, will die today for my cause," he said, shooting huge bolts of electricity down at me.

I quickly shot into the air once again, barely dodging the blast. I flipped over the man and descended toward where I had dropped my half-staff. Landing quite violently, I rolled directly over the staff, snatching it. Barely missing another blast that seemed to have been the strongest yet, I darted about to and fro, missing the electrical currents flowing around me.

I sprang into the air once more and landed on a small crosswalk that connected the two sides of a giant room. I ran toward the left side of the room, as the man fired his next string of electrical waves. I jumped quickly from the crosswalk, and the portion I leaped from exploded into thousands of tiny pieces. Being that I was quite close to the far side, the heavy crosswalk feel slowly to the floor. It wasn't long before the whole structure was smashed against the floor. Dust from the aftermath filled the air.

I noticed that Smirneth and Avin were still busy with several of the creatures, but they seemed to be doing all right. I had my hands full with the wizard. I saw him making his way toward me, and I quickly ran to the fallen structure. The old wizard followed.

"Give up, boy; you don't have a chance."

Suddenly I had an idea. The element of surprise had worked quite well thus far. I quickly shot toward the far entrance and into the darkness of the hall. I couldn't sense the wizard's presence, and that put me at a disadvantage. I had to use logic to defeat him rather than magic, and I had received my fair share of that as well.

I quickly wandered from room to room to avoid the man, but I wasn't quite sure if I was avoiding him at all, because I didn't know where he was.

"Come out, boy. Do you want to be remembered as a hiding coward or a brave man that went down fighting?"

I knew as well as he did that this was a ploy. I also knew there was a thin line between stupidity and bravery. I couldn't beat him that way, so I kneeled down to wait for him to make mistake, and then I would make my move.

I thought to myself for a few minutes as I listened to him make idle threats from somewhere in the hall. I needed a way to restrain him, but how? Then I noticed something brilliant in the dark room. It was what appeared to be a giant pendulum. It was hanging in the other side of the room, and it appeared to be part of some sort of machine. With great haste, I rounded up a small shard that was lying on the floor and a long piece of wire that was connected to part of another machine. I fused the two components together and melted the end of the wire to the cold, steel floor. All I had to do now was wait.

A few minutes passed, and I decided to encourage him a bit. So I threw a book that was lying near me against the back wall. He come flying rapidly into the room. As he passed me, I jumped out from behind the table and hurled the shard through his right thigh. He screamed out in pain and anger, tugging at the shard. It seemed to have broken his concentration.

"Damn you!" he screamed, shooting a single blast at me. I quickly dodged it, jumping into the air. I performed a single flip and disarmed the pendulum with a solitary blast of light energy. He didn't even notice as the giant ball went flying down at him. It smacked him right in the chest, and the shard was ripped from his leg as the man fell from the ball after crashing into the wall.

I walked back to where he lay on the floor, barely breathing, and the wound on his leg was squirting blood profusely. I stood over him for few seconds before he noticed me.

"You will die, boy," he said, spitting out a mouthful of blood.

"Not today," I said quietly, as he fell silent and breathless.

I ran quickly back toward the main room to find Smirneth and Avin chasing down the final creature. This last one seemed to know that he was beat, and he was running off quickly. Once he was within a few yards of me, I produced my staff and shot him dead in his tracks.

"Well," Avin said, walking up slowly, "nice to see you. What happened?"

"I had to fight that old man. He was resistant to magic, but I got him finally."

"Oh, really?" Avin said, drawing his staff in a defensive motion.

I turned to find the man running toward me frantically with the same blood-soaked shard of metal that had been in his leg. Faster than the blink of an eye, Smirneth stepped in front of me and decapitated the man in his steps. His head rolled off into the shadows, and his lifeless body fell to the ground.

"Never leave a black wizard with a head, no matter if he is dead."

"Right. I didn't know that one."

As Smirneth walked over to view the body of the man, the sound of slow clapping started to fill the room.

"Bravo, gentleman. Good show," said a voice from the shadows. Out stepped a man who appeared to stun both Avin and Smirneth.

"Caspin," Avin said in a shocked voice.

"Yes, boys, and I must say you brilliantly lead the Oriphate here, and you all fought a valiant battle. Too bad it was all in vain."

"What do you mean, Caspin? You are supposed..."

"To be in the Outer World. Well, no—lied about that."

"What's going on, you traitor?" Avin said drawing his staff.

"Seravin, don't be so quick to judge, and I assure you that staff will do you no good."

Suddenly the ground beneath us started to shake. Every few seconds another pulse of vibrations would shake the ground beneath us. Something big was about to enter the room.

A few seconds late, a creature emerged from the far end of the room. It was a dragon.

The Dragon and the Girl

The greenish scaled creature was a bit larger than an elephant with a ten-foot tail that slithered slowly behind it. It rose up not five yards from us and expanded its massive wings. It let out a gigantic scream and went back down on all fours.

"Remarkable," Smirneth said to himself.

"Don't worry, he won't attack unless I instruct him to. Now let's get down to business."

"What business?" Avin asked angrily.

"I seem to be in quite a position. You see, I have been untruthful with you all."

"Oh, really?" Smirneth said eagerly.

"Yes. I seem to have come across a stone that Smirneth wants a great deal, but it had been in my possession for quite sometime until someone so rudely stole it from me a few weeks ago."

"That stone is and always will be mine. I built it."

"Well, Smirneth, what you don't know is that the stone is a great deal more powerful than you or Dimms ever realized."

"I've had enough of this," Avin said, drawing his staff.

"Avin, don't."

"Silence."

Caspin shot a beam of black light from his hand, knocking Avin clean over the dragon.

"Caspin, what you have done to acquire that? The black fire, that is."

"Smirneth, did you ever bother to read up on the cult that practiced their witchcraft here before the flux opened?"

"No. There was no knowledge to be gained from such studies."

"That is where you are wrong. It seems that they actually had some really good ideas."

"You're insane."

"Hear me out. The group always interested me as did their rituals. I started reading about them and their beliefs, but that wasn't enough. So, I came out here and found the man you just killed. He was in some worse shape when I found him, but he got better, and I started spending a great deal of time with him."

"That was your first mistake."

"No, that was my first brilliant maneuver. He told me of things you wouldn't believe, but the most remarkable thing he ever told me about was the Sarcrain Uptake."

"Yes."

"Well, it seems that this ritual was their next course of action, after opening the flux, but you see what happened when they did that, so it was postponed, I guess you could say. This ritual would allow anyone to drain the energy from a random dimension."

"So you are going to destroy the Third Dimension. You can't!"

"But son, I'm not. You are going to do it for me, just as these fools have helped me."

"No, I would never do that. You can't make me."

"You see, the man told me about the Oriphate years before Dimms ever discovered your existence. He also told me of the energy source I would need to set the uptake in motion."

Avin walked up from behind and said, "If Argangal were here you would not get away with this."

"Good point, and Smirneth conveniently took care of that problem. He couldn't have done it without you, though. Smirneth also built the stone along with Dimms, and once I became a council member, I was able to monitor everything that happened in the Inner World."

"I built that stone to help this world, not destroy it."

"Come off it, Smirneth. The stone wouldn't have worked anyway. It's wrong. You were wrong."

"Liar!"

"Liar nothing. The stone would have worked perfectly, but there was a problem with it. Your calculations were wrong, and Dimms didn't even catch the mistake."

"That stone was my life's work."

"Don't feel so bad, Smirneth. It was a complicated task. After you built it, I had it stolen, and the old wizard did his preparatory spell on it and almost blew himself up. So we had to go to plan *B*.

"Killing the girl," I said quietly as I looked down.

"Yes, Oriphate, and it took us quite awhile to find her. Luckily, we found her just days before you arrived, but that stupid guardian found the stone. Too bad for him, and now, many years later and many deaths later, we have everything we need. If you will follow me, and don't bother with anything funny."

We all solemnly made our way up to the flux gate. Well, Caspin seemed quite giddy about the ordeal. He was consumed with evil. I could feel it radiating off him. I fully understood why our magic couldn't touch him. He had taken part in the dark rituals.

"Caspin, I have a question."

"Yes, Oriphate."

"How could you have done what you did to the girl and live with yourself?"

"Simple, my boy—for the power. You understand how intoxicating it feels to have the power rushing through you."

"But to torture a young girl and mutilate her body beyond recognition?"

"Oh, after a few of them it isn't so hard."

Smirneth spoke up. "You sick bastard."

"Say what you will, Smirneth, but you are no different."

"You lie."

"Oh, do I?"

Avin was silent.

We stepped into the large room, and the stone sat on a small altar in the middle of the room.

"Now we can't have Avin and Smirneth interfering, can we?" And with that, they froze in their steps.

"I can't move," Smirneth said loudly.

"Neither can I."

I turned around to see them both standing dead still, moving their heads about.

"You two will enjoy this. Now, Oriphate, I would like to introduce you to a few people. First, the other two council members, Locin and Sterps—I don't think you ever met them."

Caspin walked over to a large door and slip it open. I walked over and saw two charred corpses. The bodies inside were burnt to a crisp.

"Why, Caspin?" Smirneth asked.

"They got wise, too wise. Now the other person I want you to meet is under that sheet there."

At the far end of the room sat what appeared to be a bed. The sheet that Caspin spoke of rose up about five feet, and the figure slowly pulled it back. It was the girl! You could hardly tell now, but I knew it was she. I recognized every single marking with great detail. Her face was practically a skeleton now, and she was lost in a world she didn't deserve. Tears rolled down my face as she slowly made her way toward me, dragging her left leg.

"As soon as she kills you, Oriphate, the uptake will begin, and I will become the most powerful being in the universe."

I looked at Caspin, then at the girl, and back at Caspin. His crazy, mad eyes gazed into mine, and a disturbing, crooked smile came upon his face.

"I have to fight her."

"Not her—the creature she is about to become."

I watched her transform into a snarling, fanged beast right before my eyes. Foot-long claws shot from her huge hands as she drew back with intentions of ripping me in half.

I quickly sprang to the left, just missing the tips of those giant claws. The girl quickly swung at me again with her left claws and flipped high into the air, landing against the back wall.

As quickly as I could get down the wall, the creature had driven her claws just inches above me and below me as well.

Luckily, she had gotten her claws stuck in the wall, so I quickly shot off the wall and used all the magic inside me to blast a huge hole in the wall. Before I excited to think out a plan, I called out to Smirneth and Avin, "I'll be back."

"You can't run." called Caspin as I shot through the hole.

"She won't stop until you're dead."

A few minutes later, I was quickly making my way down a hallway that seemed to circle the tower, when she came bursting through the wall only ten feet ahead of me. I shot off an energy blast, but it didn't do any good. The creature just kept coming. I had no choice but to run back the other way. I made my way back along the hallway, now hovering to evade the monster with greater speed. I soon found myself coming upon on a dead end, just past where I had entered the hallway.

I thought to myself for a few minutes as the creature got closer, and I soon decided to go up instead of down. I blasted a hole in the ceiling above and went up. I soon found myself in a room with a high ceiling. It had to be the room above the flux entrance, and I realized that I was getting close to the top of the tower. I soared up to the ceiling and blew another hole, as the monster slowly made her way up the hill.

The next place I found myself was strange. It was much like a maze, and I hovered through the maze with great skill. I eventually came to a place in the maze that contained a small door in the ceiling. I suddenly noticed that the creature was destroying the maze, coming for me. I promptly opened the door to find a ladder, so I swiftly shot up the small space. The top of the ladder led to the outside, and I was just happy to be in the open.

The creature was making its way up the ladder, and I was desperately looking for some way to defeat the beast. I hurried down from the tower, but I felt that I was running out of time. The creature was too strong, and I needed a way to weaken her. I turned around to notice that the creature had jumped from the tower and was now flying! Somehow, the monster had grown wings and was coming at me. I quickly shot down to the roof below, barely escaping the creature's massive hands.

I watched the creature with one eye and looked around the roof with the other. Suddenly an idea popped in my head. The perfect way to weaken the monster was to hit it with something big. I ran around the roof looking for something big enough, while trying to evade the creature. Eventually, I found a rather large machine that seemed to be large enough. I tested it to make sure I could lift it, and I lifted it with ease.

The creature was quite high when I went up into the air. I yelled up to the creature and shot to the other end of the roof and down toward the ground. Of course, the girl followed and caught up with me in a matter of seconds. I swiftly shot back up, and the creature followed suit. I soared over the edge and toward the machine faster than I had ever flown before. With every bit of magic I had inside me, I flung it straight over my head. I turned around quickly to maneuver it, but I had done it with the flinging action. The creature wasn't expecting to run clean into a giant object flying ten times faster than she. The machine broke into a thousand pieces and fragments of metal, and the creature went flying over the side of the building.

I went to the edge of the building, and the creature was lying motionless on the building next door. She was weakened. Due to her weakened state, I was able to lift her. I quickly brought her back to the roof, but I could feel her getting stronger, because my grasp on her was swiftly fading. Her strength was returning at a remarkable rate. I looked around quickly and saw a ten-foot pole that appeared to be some sort of weather vane. I flew the creature over to the pole and dropped her on it. The creature screamed out. "I'm sorry," I thought to myself, but this had to be done. I repeatedly slammed the creature onto the pole until she was completely broken. I felt her spirit drain as I slammed her repeatedly, until every last ounce of heart in her was gone. I walked over to her, and she looked up at me. I could tell that she was crying a bit, and I kneeled down beside her. It was if the evil in her had gone as well. I gently ran my hand over her face.

I flew back toward the tower with the girl across my back. She was still breathing, but she didn't have long until she would be free at last—free from this curse that those evil men had put on her. I felt a little bad, but I knew it had to be done. She had been under the control of the black magic long enough, and this would put her to rest. I think she understood that it had to be done, and I also believe that she was thankful.

Soon enough we were there, and I promptly flung her through the large window directly behind Caspin. He turned around with a glazed-over look in his eyes, and a sign of fear and disbelief ran across his face.

"No, how did you? You couldn't have."

"I did. I used the surroundings to kill her, and now she is freed from your grasp. She is finally at peace."

"I'll kill you," Caspin screamed out as a blast came from behind, knocking him off his feet. Smirneth quickly came from behind and destroyed the stone with a single blast.

"Kill them all!" screamed Caspin seconds before Avin whacked his head off.

"What did he say?" Smirneth asked as pulses of footsteps started to shake the tower.

"Kill them all," I said with a shaky voice. At that exact moment, the dragon came bursting through the north wall. It let out a high-pitched scream before shooting a twenty-foot-wide blaze of liquid fire. All three of us jumped in opposite directions, barely missing the giant flames.

"Robert, get to the flux. That is all that is important now. We'll fight off the dragon!" screamed Avin.

So I hurried to the large door and went inside. The door closed behind me, and the inside door immediately opened, sucking me inside.

I must say that it was quite different from the positive flux. I found myself in a large room that appeared to be a study of some sort. There was a small coffee table in the middle of the room, a fire burning in the fireplace, and many shelves containing volumes upon volumes of books. I was surprised to find such a normal place inside the flux.

The room only had one door, and I was a little frightened to open it, not knowing what I would find on the other side. I knew I had to, though, so I did. The room led to another room, with that oh so familiar white glow. There was a girl sitting on the floor facing the opposite direction.

"Thank you for freeing me," she said calmly.

"You are the girl, aren't you?"

"It is polite to say, 'You're welcome'."

"You are welcome. I was happy to help you, but I feel bad…"

"Don't feel bad. You did what you had to do, and I am grateful. Now close your eyes."

She hadn't moved, and I was a bit uncomfortable with this suggestion.

"Why?"

"Please, just close your eyes."

So I did, and what I felt was quite pleasant. Someone was kissing me, but I was sure who it was. It couldn't have been the girl, because it happened as soon as I closed my eyes. This went on for a minute or so, and before the person stopped kissing, the girl said, "Open your eyes."

When I opened my eyes, I saw something that shocked me. It was a beautiful woman in a long, flowing dress with huge, feathered wings. The woman reached out with both hands and handed me a sword with a gold-plated handle.

"Go," she said simply, and I did. I walked back toward the door and opened it. I was automatically sucked into the void that had replaced the room behind it, and I soon found myself flying through the tower, just in time to see Avin flying through the air. I quickly flew over and caught him in my arms, still holding the sword.

Smirneth was busy dealing with the dragon, trying his best not to get burned alive. I hurriedly placed Avin on the floor, and he came to.

"Robert, you are back."

"Ya, let's kill this dragon."

He jumped up and ran toward the dragon. He quickly stabbed the dragon behind the eye, and as it turned around, its huge tail swung around, knocking Smirneth straight through the wall. I ran over and watched Smirneth crash to the ground.

Avin shot under the dragon's neck and grabbed Smirneth's sword, then jumped into the air, avoiding the flames.

"Robert, try to stab the dragon in the eyes."

I sprang into the air as a blaze of fire shot under me and came down on the dragon's head. I quickly drove the sword into his eye, as Avin ran under his neck once again, slicing the dragon's throat. The dragon didn't seem to bleed a whole lot. I pulled the sword from his head, and he raised his head quickly, throwing me off. Then the dragon moved his head to the left and knocked Avin clean through a large stained-glass window on the other side of the room.

It was up to me now. I ran quickly toward the dragon while his head was still turned and stabbed his other eye out. I quickly flipped backwards and pulled the sword from the dragon's head, as he fired off another burst of flames. He couldn't see me now, but his skin was way too tough to stab through. His eyes had come out easy, but I wasn't so sure about the skin.

I looked around the room and saw something very interesting in the far western ceiling of the room. Several yellow pipes were running along the ceiling, and that gave me an idea. First I blew a large hole in the western wall. I had to have a fast escape route if I was going to pull this off. I picked a piece of wood that was lying on the floor and threw it at the dragon, who was quite confused at the time. The dragon quickly turned as soon as the wood hit him, and he started for me. As quickly as I could, I leaped into the air and sliced two yellow pipes in half. I flew swiftly toward the hole in the wall when I heard the dragon blow his final burst of fire. As I sank down toward the woods below, the tower exploded with great force, and the chain reaction of explosions shook the whole compound. The whole place was a blazing inferno before I ever reached the trees. I eventually came to a sudden halt, hitting the cold hard ground.

When I woke up, there was a haze of smoke. I could hardly see. I soon realized that Avin was standing over me. He looked blurry, and I wasn't sure if it was because of the smoke or the tremendous fall I had taken. All three of us had fallen from the tower, and I would say it was about five stories high. Avin was quite bruised up and quite bloody. Half the blood on him probably wasn't even his, though. I wasn't even sure how I looked, but I'm sure about the same.

"You did it, Robert. The flux is gone."

"No, Avin, we all did it. I couldn't have done it without you and Smirneth," I said, slowly getting up. I was very sore.

"Where is Smirneth?"

"He's around. He is just looking at the aftermath of the explosion. I think his feelings are hurt. His life's work was a failure, and his lab had to be destroyed."

"This is his lab."

"Yes, he probably spent more time here than anywhere else. He loved this place."

"Do you still blame Smirneth for all of this?"

"No. I think Smirneth redeemed himself today. This is the act that will allow forgiveness and virtue to be restored to Smirneth. I think he has proven himself."

"I think I saw Argangal in the flux, but I am not sure. Whatever I saw had huge wings, and it looked like a woman."

"Well, Argangal did have female features, but Argangal was neither male nor female. The Statuiarns were born from stone."

"She gave me a sword. Where is it?"

"It's over here."

Avin led me to a large tree not far from where we had been standing. The beautiful sword was driven straight through the tree.

"Smirneth and I have both tried to pull it out, but it won't move an inch."

I reached up and pulled the sword from the tree as if I were pulling it through a stick of hot butter.

"Amazing."

About that time Smirneth came walking up, and he seemed a bit heartbroken. I could tell he had been crying. He looked up at us and saw that I had pulled the sword from the tree. The started expression on his face seemed to tell exactly how shocked he actually was.

"Well, Oriphate, I guess there isn't too much you can't do. You defeated two black magicians, a cursed beast, and a dragon all in the matter of an afternoon."

Then Smirneth came up and did something I never would have expected. He put his arms around me and gave me the most affectionate hug I had ever received.

"I don't know what we would have done without you, Oriphate. I am thankful for your gift."

"Well, like I told Avin, I couldn't have done it without the two of you."

That night we decided to just camp there, because it was already getting late. Avin started a small fire, and we all sat around conversing about the adventurous afternoon we had all had. We all agreed that it was the single most exciting experience of our lives, mine especially.

"I have a question. What made the girl so special? I mean, why did they have to have her?"

"Well, I am not exactly sure, but I think it has something to do with this."

Smirneth reached into his cloak and pulled out the small doll that had belonged to the girl.

"I thought that was thrown into the well."

"It was, but Avin found it when he went down to get the man out of the drain. You see, the well drains into the river."

"Yes, I found it there next to the man. I thought it looked interesting, so I brought it up along with the man."

I sat and looked at the doll for a moment, wondering how it could have had anything to do with the stone or the girl.

"I don't really understand how this doll could have made the girl special."

It seems that both Avin and Smirneth had fallen into a deep sleep, and I was alone. So I sat up next to a large tree, looking into the doll's eyes. I concentrated very hard on the doll, trying to see something.

It wasn't long before I found myself in a doll shop of some sort. It was quite large. There were all sorts of dolls in the multiple rooms. Many of the dolls were quite beautiful, with various colored dresses. Some of them were laughing and smiling, and some were not so happy. The further I got into the store, the sadder the dolls became. Some of the dolls were downright ugly.

The worst of the dolls were in the last room. Some of them had long white fangs protruding from their horrid mouths, others had yellowish teeth that were crooked and stained. Suddenly a man walked into the room, holding the doll that had belonged to the girl. He was a freaky-looking man who seemed a bit familiar, but I couldn't place him until he spoke.

"Jonen, I have brought the doll for you," he said, looking about for the owner, I suppose. It was the evil wizard. He was a great deal younger, but he spoke in the same rusty voice. Soon a man appeared out of nowhere.

"Welcome. May I see the doll first?" He took the doll in his hand, turning it about. He looked at every feature. I could tell that he knew his trade.

"Are you going to buy it or not?"

"Why are you so eager to sell such a valuable doll?"

"Because I need funds to return to the sea. I am quite broke, so please."

"Well, it is a very nice doll, but I don't exactly understand why it feels so strange. I mean, in my hands. It is giving off a strange sort of energy."

"That's just your imagination."

After that was said, I found myself back at the tree, holding the doll tightly.

Avin and I sat quietly in the same small room that I had stayed in the whole time I had been in the castle. You would think that we would have more to say to each other, seeing that it was the last time we would ever see each other, but we didn't. Avin sat, staring at the wall, and I was simply looking down. Finally the silence broke.

"Well, I guess you're quite ready to get back."

"Yes, I suppose. I am going to miss all of this. This world is so different."

"Will you miss your powers?"

"I guess, but I don't think I am ready to be this powerful all the time. I just want to go back to being plain old Robert Stevens."

"I can understand that. With great powers comes a lot of responsibility. Sometimes I wish I could go back to the wilderness and marry a nice girl and live out the rest of my life in a normal sort of way."

"Couldn't you, though? You could always give up your powers."

"I could, but I have to remain here to protect the people of this planet. This is my purpose for living. It is also what I have devoted my life to. I can't give it up. There is too much I am responsible for now."

"I understand. It is very admirable of you to be so devoted to the people here. You truly are a hero."

"You are as well."

"No, not really. I don't feel like one."

"You are just as much of a hero as any of us."

"But you actually had to work hard to get where you are now. You had to sacrifice everything to get to where you are now. My powers just came to me, and I didn't have to do anything. Don't be so quick to sell yourself short."

"I see what you are saying, but if it hadn't been for you, we would have never been able to stop the flux."

"But if it wasn't for you, I wouldn't have been brought here, and Dimms' machine brought us here. Smirneth played an important role in helping as well."

"So your point is that we did it together."

"Yes. You see, we all worked together to accomplish this. Not one of us was more important than the other, because we all played a crucial role in saving both our worlds. If it hadn't been for you and Smirneth, I would have never been able to accomplish a thing."

"Robert, you are a very noble person, and I don't mean as the Oriphate. Putting that aside, you are a wonderful person, powers or not."

Thank you," I said, once again looking down. We had spoken our peace, and silence fell over the campsite.

ROBERT'S RETURN TO THE THIRD DIMENSION

Later that afternoon, Avin and I sat in the lab as Dimms prepared the machine. He said it would take some time to prepare the machine, because he had to put me back at the exact time I left. He had told me, if I happened to get back before I was pulled into the flux, just stay out of sight until everything was finished. I hoped that would not happen, though, because I feared something would go wrong.

There was a huge chance that something would go wrong. Dimms was a brilliant man, and I had full confidence in him. He scurried about, turning various knobs, pushing buttons, and reading different values on the many screens that came on and went off as he walked around. He was busy at work, and anyone could tell that he knew exactly what he was doing. I couldn't possibly understand how anyone could run such a complicated machine.

"It won't be long now. I just have to put in a few more formulas and let them run, and it will be ready. I have to be very careful, though, because one mistake could pt you anywhere in the Third Dimension at any time."

I didn't like the sound of that. What if I ended up in the prehistoric times running from dinosaurs and cavemen? Then I thought to myself, Dimms put Avin there once before, so this wasn't that much different.

It wasn't long before Dimms joined us. He explained that it wouldn't be long now, and we would just have to wait. We all said our last good-byes as the machine came to full power.

"Well, it is time, Robert. If you will go up to the podium and await the vortex, I'll start it. As soon as the red light above the vortex gets to the last mark, just step in."

"All right." I walked up the steps toward the hole in the wall that would soon be a glowing bright yellow. I slowly waited for the vortex to come to power. It took some time, but it started just as it always did. The small speck of light soon appeared, and it continued to get bigger. I watched the red light slowly move up the line toward the end.

I leisurely turned around to wave good-bye to Avin, and noticed that Smirneth was standing behind him. Neither Dimms nor Avin had seen him. I waved and Avin waved back. Funny thing was that Smirneth didn't wave. The next thing that Smirneth did alarmed me quite a bit. He pulled his wand from his cloak and shot the largest blaze of energy I had seen straight through the ceiling. Avin quickly turned and pulled his wand as well. I jumped down just in time to see a large piece of equipment fall from the ceiling and crush Dimms and the portion of the machine he had been operating. Avin turned to watch Dimms be crushed.

"No!" He ran over to where Dimms was, and I jumped down from the platform. The red light quickly decreased, and the growing vortex disappeared.

"What have you done, Smirneth, why?" Avin said jumping up.

"I am simply following orders. You must understand why I had to do this. It is the only way."

"Orders from who? You killed Dimms. He's dead. I don't understand at all." I could tell that Avin was fighting back tears. I was simply speechless.

"Smirneth was simply doing what he was told, Seravin. We figured it would be hard for you comprehend." It was Fargin, the senior council member. He stood with a solemn look on his face.

"Why?" I asked. "Why kill Dimms?"

"Because we knew that Dimms would never allow us to keep you here, Robert."

"Robert is not staying here. He has to go back to the Third Dimension where he belongs."

Stay here, but why? I thought about for a few minutes, in the midst of all that was going on around me, and realized that it wouldn't have been such a problem. Why couldn't they have just asked?

"I would have considered staying, Smirneth. This was the wrong way to do this—can't you see that?"

"I wasn't sure if you would agree with what I had in mind."

"What's that?"

"We don't need you; we just need your body. To study, that is."

"No, Smirneth, you can't do that."

"Think of it, donating your body to research that could possibly save millions again someday. Maybe even save your dimension once more."

Fargin walked closer and spoke once more, "Avin, please don't make this any hard than it already is. This first stone, as you know, didn't work properly. What if another group of idiots open another flux? We need Robert here, as does his dimension. This could happen many more times."

"No, I don't understand. How could you kill Dimms, Smirneth? He was your friend. He defended you when no one else would."

"It is just part of natural order, Avin. It had to be done. Think of it as a mistake if you wish. Heron didn't think it was a good idea either, and he was persuaded to leave. I knew Dimms would see this the same way as you do, and I will kill you again if I have to."

"You cold hearted..."

"Never mind all that, Avin. You are going to cooperate or join Dimms."

"I would rather join him than betray him!"

With that, Avin quickly shot Fargin, knocking him off his feet. As soon as he did this, Smirneth shot a blast of light energy at me, and I quickly sprang into the air.

"Robert get to the south end of the lab, and restart the gyroscope. It is your only change. You only have a five-minute window."

Smirneth swiftly fired again, this time at Avin, but Avin jumped into the air as well. The blast barely missed him and went on to take out another portion of the lab. Sparks and debris flew all around. I took off for the sound end of the lab, but Smirneth wasn't far behind.

Smirneth was coming in close, and it was all I could do to evade him. Avin wasn't far behind. Smirneth soon fired off another shot that grazed my leg. He caught up with me as we turned the corner. He violently pulled me to the floor, and we both smashed into it with great force. Avin was there before we had a chance to collect ourselves.

"Smirneth, to believe I actually thought you had changed. You are no better than Caspin."

"You dare not say that!" Smirneth screamed, shooting a fiery ball at Avin. Avin quickly blocked it and produced a dual blast of light energy from both eyes.

"Avin!" I screamed out as Smirneth landed next to me. I quickly pulled the giant sword I had received in the flux from inside my cloak and threw it to Avin.

"Go, I'll hold him off."

"I can't leave you like this."

"You must." As Avin said this I got a sudden glimpse of a figure behind him. It was Fargin. Fargin stepped up and stabbed Avin straight through the abdominal region. I watched the bloody sword come through Avin, and Fargin quickly pulled it out. Avin immediately fell dead.

"Noooooooo!"

Instead of being sad, I grew very angry. Fargin looked up at me and smiled. Smirneth was up now, but he wasn't up for long. I quickly let out a sonic burst of sound energy from my mouth that sent both Smirneth and Fargin to the floor. The whole room shook for a few minutes. I ran over and grabbed the sword from Avin's hands. Fargin was getting up when I came down upon him with great force, severing his head.

It seems that Smirneth was up as well, but he was a bigger challenge. He had already gone to the air. He shot several blasts with his wand, but I quickly dodged the first two and blocked the third with my sword.

"You cannot win, boy. It is no use."

I quickly heaved the sword at Smirneth and turned away. I knew as well as he did that I was running out of time, so I was off again. He quickly tailed me, though, but my anger was fueling my departure. Smirneth continued to shoot at me, but I couldn't be hit. I could soon see the door to the gyroscope, but it started to close before I was within fifty feet of it. I dashed as quickly as a bullet and just made it before the door closed. Smirneth came to a sudden halt, smashing into the door.

I rapidly restarted the gyroscope, hoping it would work. The timer said I only had twenty-seven seconds to restart it, and I just made it with eight left. The giant machine started to turn, and it was quite slow at first. It quickly gained momentum, and huge bolts of electrical energy filled the room. All the while Smirneth tried to break through the door.

It wasn't long before the giant vortex appeared above the machine, and I could feel it pulling me closer. I was shocked several times as I was pulled through the air toward the giant light. It pulled me closer and closer, and it wasn't long before I was flying through the void.

It had only been about twenty seconds or so, and I could feel that something wasn't right. The vortex was losing momentum, and I had slowed down considerably. That is when something grabbed me from behind. It was Smirneth! He had come into the void with me.

"I destroyed the gyroscope, you little fool. You should have stayed."

"You are crazy!" I screamed as we struggled.

"No, you are crazy. Now you will never see your family again, your world again, anything again!"

We struggled as we flew through the void. The intensity of the vortex grew stronger and stronger. We were nearing the end. Smirneth quickly produced his wand, but I managed to take it from him. With all the energy I had, I stabbed the wand into his neck. He screamed out once and let go of me. He fell a few feet behind as we quickly neared the end.

The blaze of light grew stronger and quickly spit us both out. Smirneth and I flew through the air and eventually landed in a small lake of some sort. Apparently, Smirneth was denser than water, because he quickly sank to the bottom; however, I slowly swam to the edge of the lake.

The place where we ended up was pleasant, or so it seemed. It was much like a prairie of some sort. There was tall, dry, browning grass growing as far as you could see. I decided to walk on, and I soon found a small dirt road. It wasn't long before a wagon came into view. It was coming my way. There was an older gentleman driving three horses, all of which were quite elegant.

"Well, hello there. Can I help you?" the man said very politely.

"Yes, where am I?"

"You're about ten miles south of Lincoln, Nebraska. I was just headed up there to pay off some debts. Can I give you a ride?"

I got up on the wagon and sat down next to the man. I didn't have a streak of magical powers. I had lost them all.

"Damn, boy, you look like you been through a war zone. I think you need a doctor."

"No, I'm fine. I have to ask you another question, and it is going to sound strange, but I need to know what year it is."

"Why, it's 1873. Where the hell have you been?"

"You wouldn't believe me if I told you. Hey, one more thing."

"Yeah?"

"You wouldn't happen to have a cigarette would you?"

The man handed me a cigarette that appeared to be hand-rolled. He lit it with a sharp-smelling match, and I sat smoking it, wondering what I needed to do. Simply, there was nothing to do about this. I started to question whether or not I should have died, like my father did. Would it have made me more of a hero? Had I really done anything at all? After all, I did save the Third Dimension, but I couldn't save Avin. I felt terrible about that.

The man seemed a bit unnerved by me, so I asked him to let me off. I walked up toward a small thicket of trees and brush and sat down on a rock. I sat there and watched the sunset. It was the most beautiful sunset I had ever seen. The horizon was a bright shade of red for the longest time, but it eventually faded to darkness, and night fell upon me.